Runaway:
Selene Ryder #1
By Samantha Allard

This is a work of fiction. Similarities to real people, places, or events are entirely coincidental.

RUNAWAYS

First edition. June 25, 2022.

Copyright © 2022 Samantha Allard.

ISBN: 979-8201762889

Written by Samantha Allard.

Samantha Allard

Guild Story:
Heartless
The Firestones
Selene Ryder:
Runaways
Spells and Scales:
The Wizard of Black Hollow
The Ghosts in the Glades
The Merfolk of Sirena

Chapter One

I crossed my arms and glared at the building opposite me. The crumbling brick work. The streetlamps hadn't worked in months. The broken window which Joseph Barlowe hadn't bothered to fix because of 'reasons' and had instead covered it with long slats of wood. To complete the look the glaring neon sign advertised girls who stripped from eight till late. The Golden Eagle or as the staff called it, the place dreams went to die wasn't a classy place. The clientele went there for the girls and the watered-down whiskey.

And I hated it.

It shouldn't have been possible to hate a building but every time I turned the corner and saw it, the sight of it turned my stomach. I hated everything about it. The smell of unwashed bodies and cigarette smoke seeped into my clothes and never washed out again. The patrons never looked higher than a girl's chest and liked to get grabby with the staff. I'd lost count of the number of times I had to stop myself from reacting. Hell, I would have preferred to be strapped into a chair with a one-eyed man armed with a scalpel and that was from experience. I absentmindedly rubbed my jaw. At least some scars healed.

"You're going to have to go in there at some point," I muttered to myself. With a grunt, I pushed myself away from the wall and crossed the street. The car park was mostly empty and surrounded by a hedge. I moved between a gap in the hedge, checked the road, and pushed the front doors open.

A steady under-beat of music filled the bar, and I blinked a few times to adjust to the darkness. The dancers strutted across the round stages and did something that resembled dancing coupled with the odd twirl around the poles built in the center. The pay was good since they got to keep half of their tips. The bar staff didn't have the same luxury. All our tips, if we got them, went into a pot. The gargoyle upstairs took his cut and then we could split it between the staff on duty. Overall, it wasn't worth it, but we put up with a lot of bullshit for a payday.

The whole place made my skin crawl. Customers watched the girls like they weren't anything better than meat who could dance or at least gyrate against cold steel. To a point it nearly made me wish for my old job. There were about a hundred guys in tonight and in a small bar that ate up a lot of space. I weaved my way through the crowd. How did I end up in this place? A question I asked myself a lot. It boiled down to something simple. I didn't have a choice. The life I left behind wasn't something I could put down on a resume. Someone's hand brushed against my jean-clad ass, and I glared over my shoulder. The urge to break the drunken man's fingers nearly overwhelmed me. He visibly went white and spluttered out an apology as I stalked away.

Fluent in three languages. I could assemble a sniper rifle blindfolded and I was stuck here. The price of invisibility. My punishment for the sins I'd committed in the name of what I'd been told was right. I kept myself under the radar because I didn't want my past to track me down and drag me out of bed one night. Nothing linked me to the life I left behind. If it meant I had to work in this hellhole, I could deal with it. It beat the alternative.

A few of the regulars sat at the bar staring into pints of beer. Men on either of them side waved money to get the attention of the staff. It was annoying as hell but they didn't care. They were mostly workers from the building sites. When I first started to work at the Golden Eagle it had been mostly surrounded by deserts. Deserted and desolate. It brought in bikers and men who spent their welfare checks. Now someone had the bright idea to build casinos on the land. They were trying to inject new life into the area. It brought in a new clientele but there was something about the land and buildings which seeped the life out of its workers.

It was the last place Blue Isis would think to look for me.

Three years with no incidents. I almost believed they stopped searching for me. Almost. I could have sold my skill set to the highest bidder, but I didn't want that life anymore. If I was okay with killing people I would have stayed with Blue Isis. No, I wanted freedom and this place offered something close to it.

I ducked underneath the bar. The staff looked frazzled. It hadn't been a good night, but if I managed to get through the shift without wanting to put a bullet into anyone, I considered it a victory.

"Is it too much to ask we keep the bar stocked? You know, we're a bar. We should at least have the basics." A familiar voice cuts through the noise. I didn't even have to glance across to recognize the snarky tones of my roommate.

"People didn't come here to hear you complain." Another one of the bartenders snapped back.

Nicki Rose snorted. She rested her hands on her hips, her blonde hair was brushed up in a bun on top of her head. "Yeah, they came for the beer. It doesn't look like they're going to be getting much of that either."

"Sell the bottles then. I'll change the barrel when I get a moment to breathe. You know when Hell freezes over."

Nicki swore under her breath. Nobody liked working here but they never came out and said it. Nikki never sweet-coated her dislike for the bar, the patrons, or the people who worked there.

She glanced up and gave me a little wave before she took the money from the customer and flashed them a smile. Nicki had attitude in spades, but she was normal and nowhere near as psychotic as some of the people I'd left behind. It raised an interesting question though. What did I bring to our friendship besides half of the rent? Oh yeah, my sparkling wit and charm. I fought against the urge to roll my eyes. It wasn't easy to adjust to a normal life. Some of my training still managed to leak through which helped when I needed to deal with the little golem who resided upstairs in the office.

There were several perfect words to describe Joseph Barlowe, tight-fisted, slimy, and disgusting were the usual suspects. He'd rather make money than spend it. It was the reason he thought he could get away with running the club with a skeleton crew.

It was either going to put some of his staff into an early grave or him.

I shrugged off my jacket and ignored the unimpressed glances cast my way because of my jeans. Joseph preferred his girls in short skirts. He said the uniform brought in more money. If I wanted to flash my panties every time I bent over, I'd dance on one of the stages. The only time I'd worn a skirt, a customer had grabbed my ass. The guy had been lucky he'd left with a sprained wrist. It's why I kept a fair distance between myself and the clientele, which usually meant I worked behind the bar.

The staff thought I didn't get fired because I had something over Joseph or had gotten under him. The truth was I knew most of his dirty little secrets. The bar would be closed with the things I knew. The little rat infestation. The fact the food was barely fit for human consumption. The things the dancers did for extra money. He lived in fear that one day I'd follow through on one of my threats.

I'd barely hung my jacket up when a girl called out my name. "Selene, Joseph wants to talk to you before you start." The girl who'd spoken was tall, blonde, and rubbed the tip of her nose like a bad habit. It had to be whatever drugs she took to get through her shift. Some had flasks hidden away. Others sniffed the white stuff. I just brought my usual charm and wit. It worked for me. Also, drugs weren't a clever idea for me. I couldn't risk losing control.

"Brilliant, what does he want?" I preferred to get through my shift with as little contact with the troll as possible. One of these days he'd push me too far and he wasn't worth going on the run again.

"Don't know and don't care. Just be quick." She flicked her ponytail over her shoulder and went back to ignoring me. She wasn't as scary as she thought she was. My path had crossed with people much scarier than her. People didn't bother me during my shifts. I didn't work in the hellhole to make friends.

I walked down the corridor, navigating my way around the boxes of alcohol pushed up against the walls. The lights in the staff room were off and I didn't bother to check the door. Joseph kept the keys in the office and none of the girls wanted to be left alone with him. There was something about being in a room with Joseph which made me wish for a hot shower and a scrubbing brush. Even I wasn't an exception. Joseph wouldn't dare to try and touch me. He was a slime ball, but he had a survival streak a mile wide. The only difference between me and the girl was I could kill him with a well-placed spoon. Hell, I wouldn't even need a weapon.

I made my way up the steps to the dark blue door at the top. He never left his office and the day he did, well I'd have to check the temperature in hell. The sound of his chair creaking under the strain of his weight reached me through the wooden panel. I glanced up at the camera which hung on the top right hand of the ceiling. It moved from side to side as if it had a life of its own. A few sharp taps to the door and I marked the time he made me wait in my head. I crossed my arms and started to hum the alphabet song. After a few exceptionally long seconds he barked out an order which echoed around the tight space.

Fighting against the urge to roll my eyes, I pushed open the door. I hated this room. I think I would be hard-pressed to find anything about the place I liked. Against the left wall was the feed from the cameras set up around the bar. Underneath the desk were the computer towers. The locked cabinet on the right was the home to the discs of the recordings. Joseph was a small, squat man—more gargoyle than human—with a face only a mother could love. He'd look right at home hidden under some bridge terrorizing goats. There might have been a chin there at one point, but now it was swallowed up by rolls of fat. Even with the comb-over, there was no mistaking the ever-expanding bald spot highlighted underneath the lights.

"What do you want, Joseph? They need me downstairs."

The smile he gave me made me want to punch him. Something about him brought out all my more violent tendencies. "You've kept secrets, Lene."

The way he shortens my name made my stomach twist uncomfortably. He felt brave and warning bells went off in my head. "Do you want to get to the point? I've got work to do. You know, the thing you pay me for?"

He licked his bottom lip. Slobber remained behind, leaving it as wet and as shiny as his hair. It reminded me of how dogs look when they've found a juicy bone. "You didn't put your real name on the application."

My stomach dove to the soles of my boots. I'd been safe for three years. The Blue Isis—the branch of the government who'd trained me—hadn't even found me here, but this jackass managed to find out I used an alias? "What are you talking about?"

He smirked. "Does the name Ruby Williams sound familiar? I've got a feeling you'll want to keep it buried. Since you went to such an effort to hide it in the first place."

The name caught my attention. I had to be dreaming. I'd had nightmares about someone finding out my real identity. Even the mere mention of it left me feeling physically sick. There was no way he'd let this go. He thought he finally had something on me, something he could use to get whatever he wanted from me, and I had a good idea what it was. My body went tense as instinct tried to take over. No, I couldn't use my ability here. At least not yet. One thing was certain: this wasn't going to end well—for him.

"What do you want?" I didn't see any point in denying it.

"I'm sure we can come up with an arrangement." The way he looked over me made my skin crawl again and left me in no doubt about what he hinted at with the subtly of a sledgehammer. I swallowed past the sickness that welled in my throat. I'd rather bash myself to death with my arm.

"Is it worth that?"

Another leer and this time he rubbed his stomach like an overweight Buddha. With a belly so big he hadn't seen his dick in a long time. "All you need to know is I own your ass." He licked his bottom lip again. "I'm sure you'll be creative. You've got until the end of your shift, or I forward this information on."

I spun on my heel and left Joseph to his perverse thoughts. It would be easier to leave and never look back. I'd done it before, but curiosity made me stay. The need to find out how Joseph discovered my secret overran my instincts to run.

One thing was certain though. Joseph wouldn't live to see the morning. The thought made me happier than I liked. If there was anyone who deserved an untimely end it was him.

Chapter Two

The name Ruby Williams held no good memories for me. I didn't feel bad when I dropped it, choosing the name Selene Ryder instead. Blue Isis had trained me to be a killer. The final test had pitted me against a fellow operative, a friend. Lisa Evans had been able to manipulate air. I thought of her sometimes. Her laugh. The way the skin between her eyes crinkled whenever she tried to focus without her glasses. She'd been sweet. My first real friend. Then Blue Isis told us we would have to fight until one of us was dead. All my flaws. The human part I'd still managed to keep hidden from Blue Isis but not from her, had all become a weakness she could exploit. In the end, neither of us had wanted to die, and neither wanted to fight the other person but we knew. Only one of us would be walking away from the training area. It was either her or me. I touched my jaw caught up in the memory. Lisa fought dirty. A tightness in my chest told me she tried to pull the air out of my lungs. Vision slightly blurred. I had to put her down fast. One telekinetic enhanced punch to the jaw and her head snapped to the side. She crumpled to the ground like a puppet with its strings cut. I ended up breaking her neck. That night changed me. Instead of being the student, the trainee, I became a killer. Murdering got easier over time. I buried the part of me which remembered being anything else. I became closed off, cold inside. Then my last assignment happened. I went from being the loyal little worker bee to always looking over my shoulder.

A scream. A little girl calling out for her mother. A mother who would never hear her daughter's voice again because I put a bullet inside of her. The sight of the girl uselessly shaking her mother's limp arm haunted me.

"Sweetheart, you okay?" Nicki's voice cut through my dark thoughts, and I stopped cleaning the floor.

I shook my head, but the memory held fast. "I'm fine, why?"

She smiled. It was a rare sight in a place like this. Nicki deserved better, but then we all did. "You've been mopping the same section for a few minutes. Is it about Joseph? What did he say to you? Believe me, whatever he said is bullshit. We all work hard, and we deserve more of those tips he likes to hoard up in his cave."

"Oh, it's nothing like that just, 'I can break down the carefully crafted lie which is your life,' I muttered under my breath. "You know Joseph. He's an asshole on any day ending in a Y." I glanced up at the cameras around the bar and fought the urge to flip my middle finger at them.

He thought he was the king of his little empire, a cheap place with dancers dead behind the eyes. It truly boggled the mind.

Nicki laughed before she leaned closer to whisper, "He might change, but I think hell will freeze over first." She glanced over her shoulder, but the back bar was empty. The lights had been dimmed and most of the girls had either sat down or left. Normal people hated Joseph, a few however didn't mind kissing his ass if they thought it would get them ahead. She leaned the brush she'd been using against the wall. "You want to walk home together?"

"I've got some paperwork to fill out before he'll let me leave. That was what Joseph wanted to talk to me about." I couldn't tell her goodbye. A part of me wanted to say the words. I owed her that much, how quickly it would all fall apart. Secret identities, government agencies, and tonight would be Joseph's last, none of those things sounded believable. Well, except the last one. A smile tugged at my lips.

I still needed to head home first. I kept a few things hidden in a box underneath the floorboards in my room. Thankfully, Nicki slept like the dead, so she wouldn't hear me coming and going.

She frowned. "He couldn't have got you to do that earlier?"

I shrugged and told her something vaguely believable. "We were busy earlier. You know how much Joseph hates us not taking money."

She laughed and I broke out in a real grin. "Okay, I'll be in bed when you get home anyway. I'll see you in the morning. I'll make breakfast." Nicki gave me a half-wave and disappeared through the side door.

Not for me, you won't. Sadness wells in my chest.

I didn't bother to finish cleaning the floor. Instead, I put the mop and bucket away into its cabinet, more out of habit than any real desire to tidy up. The buzz of the cameras moving reached my ears without the busy bar noise interfering with it. There was no doubt in my mind Joseph watched my every step. I didn't like the way anticipation built in the pit of my stomach. It had been three years since I killed someone, but my body knew what it needed to do. I mentally went to a place that didn't care.

A part buried a long time ago. One I wished had stayed dead.

I PUSHED THE WHITE door open and walked into the little troll's den. It looked like Joseph hadn't moved from his seat since I saw him last. The man had laziness down to a fine art.

He swirled around in his chair and the way he cast his gaze over me, missing my face completely, I fought against the urge to rub my arms. I'd met some real scumbags in my days at Blue Isis. Killed a few of them and had to work with the rest. Joseph thought he was the big dog, he was just a sick puppy. "I knew you'd come around to my idea of thinking." Drool practically oozed from his lips, and he brushed the back of his hand against it leaving a trial against his cheek.

I rested my hands on my hips and fixed him with a stare that would have made lesser men tremble. Joseph was missing the survival gene as his gaze drifted back down to my chest. "Are you going to tell me what you know?"

He rubbed his hands across the front of his trousers. "I know your name and the fact you're a popular girl. I bet you don't want the group you worked for knowing you're here."

Well, he was right about that. They made me a monster. I'd rather die than go back. "Who else have you told?" I walked toward him with a deliberate sway of my hips. Being sexy or seductive wasn't what I was known for, but I needed him to relax, to let down his guard. I certainly wouldn't have guessed my night would end this way. With a disgusting human being who made my skin crawl and my lunch want to make a return trip. "There's no point in doing this if you have. Unless you think I'm going to sleep with your friends as well." A shudder went through me. I didn't plan on sleeping with him, but Joseph struck me as a man who would get off the idea of using me as a personal toy.

"Now, that's a thought." He was short enough that his gaze was level with my breasts. He reached for them; sweat glistened on his palms. My stomach turned at the thought of him touching me and I pushed him away until he went back down into the chair. Air left him in an audible whoosh as he connected with the leather.

"Don't you want me to be creative to buy your silence?" I teased and imagined his head popping like a balloon. "I've been thinking about this all shift." I try to make my voice seductive, a purr I hadn't mastered but which had the desired effect. I rested my hands on his shoulders. "Let me do it my way."

His watery blue eyes widen, and he nodded. I reached down with invisible fingers and stroked the power that was my telekinesis. I'd been born with the gift and even if it hadn't been used since I left Blue Isis, the power remained close. If I called for it, it would answer me. The thought brought me comfort. I tugged on his silk tie. He squeaked like a mouse the moment it became trapped. I yanked hard on it and his eyes bulged like a goldfish.

"I'm going to ask you this once. Where did you put the information?"

There was a moment when the expression on his face changed from surprised to *oh fuck*. He was screwed and not in the way he'd hoped. My inner power welled over me, and I smiled as Joseph tried to tug away from me.

As I pulled on the tie again, his face turned a wonderful shade of purple. "I'm sure if you knew anything important about me you would have known blackmailing me was stupid. Not if you want to keep breathing."

Joseph shuddered, clawing at my hands, desperate for air. I loosened my grip a little. I might have hated him, but I needed him alive to answer my questions.

It happened quickly. A sharp pressure against my chest and I tumble backward. Pain erupted at the back of my skull and suddenly I can't focus. The printer had left a dent in my head. Tears sprang to my eyes. He'd caught me by surprise. It had been a rookie mistake and it cost me.

"You're a stupid bitch. I'm going to make you feel pain before they take you." He wheezed the words at me as he tried to catch his breath.

He pushed my knees apart and started to undo my jeans. When he tried to force his hand beneath the waistband of my pants, I screamed out in rage, but he slaps his hand against my mouth. Pain throbbed at the base of my skull makes it impossible to focus my telekinesis. I tried to push him off me. Joseph was a small man, but he'd pinned me against the floor and the printer. I opened my mouth wider and swiftly sank my teeth into his thumb. A slap across the face and my face explodes in a red haze of pain.

The stars flashing before my eyes multiplied. If he hit me again I'd start seeing planets. A chill washed over my bared legs, and I screamed again. In a split second, my blurred vision came back into sharp focus. I darted my gaze toward Joseph and hissed, "Stop."

My telekinesis snapped out of me like a whip and held him still. I caught the faint tremble in the air which covered him like a shimmering cocoon. It didn't take much effort to keep him still. My years of training with Blue Isis meant I had it down to a fine art even if it had taken me a while to unleash it. Joseph tried to move. There was the barest push to the telekinetic bubble. I smiled at the precise moment he realized he wasn't going anywhere. It wasn't a nice smile.

"You're lucky I don't have time for this bullshit, because for this little stunt of yours? There are things I could do to you that would make you wish I just killed you." I growled the words at him and tugged my jeans back up. Anger filled every part of me like a white-hot rage. The truth was it wasn't Joseph I was angry with.

You know better than this, Selene. You never meet a mark in an enclosed space where he has the advantage. You never draw it out. I should have knocked him out as soon as I walked into the room and searched his computers.

I continued to silently berate myself as I stalked past him and in one swift motion, unhooked the keyboard in front of his computer and used the back of his head for batting practice.

He grunted as he hit the ground.

I knelt next to the computer tower. My head throbbed in time with my heart. There was enough power left in me for one short burst. Afterward, it would be a lot harder to call on my telekinesis. I placed my hands on either side of it. Metal cracked as the pieces broke down. It took a few minutes for me to reduce the entire computer tower to the size of a small cube. I slipped it into my pocket before I retrieved the security tapes, snapped them in half, and pulled out the flimsy film.

There was no way I planned on leaving any evidence behind. I glanced at Joseph over my shoulder and smiled grimly.

There were two options.

I could kill him.

Or I could leave him for Blue Isis. They weren't going to be happy to find the girl he'd promised them was gone because he couldn't keep his dick in his pants.

"You're going to wish I killed you."

Chapter Three

As I left by the side entrance for the last time cold air hit me like a blast of icy rain water. I wasn't thrilled I needed to go on the run again, but no part of me was upset to see the back of another place I hated. As the frigid air encroached through the layers of my clothing, I pulled up the hood of my jacket and buried my hands into the deep pockets. It wasn't enough. My body shivered hard enough my teeth rattled.

I should have brought a scarf.

As agents for Blue Isis, we'd been taught never to relax, never to let our guard down, and because of that training, I'd made sure to have a backup plan. I'd just wished it never would be needed. The money stashed under the floorboards in my room could have been used a million times over. I'd lived on the breadline for months when my pay had been short. Survived on toast and cups of coffee. Even during the worse time, I hadn't touched it. In my darkest moments. The days I hated my job the most. The days I wish I could have walked out. I never did it. I knew there was a market for my skills, but I never sunk that low. Redemption wasn't supposed to be easy. If it was all the monsters would be doing it.

Everything was black except for the random streetlamps and stars that dotted the dark sky. The shift ended hours ago, but I still needed to get home, grab the money, and kill some time before the first train out of here left. I was halfway across the parking lot when I noticed the van, the only thing in the otherwise empty car park. Apprehension filled every part of me with nervous energy. Something was wrong. There was no reason for the van to be there, highlighted by the stark light created by the streetlamps. A glance told me there wasn't anywhere to hide. The line of trees to the forest was too far away and the hedges around the car park kept everything contained. I was trapped.

Fuck.

The hair at the nape of my neck stood up, but the warning came too late. With barely enough time to think about escape routes, the doors on the van swung open. Two men stepped out. It might have been a few years, but the uniform hadn't changed. Nondescript dark suits made it easy for them to fade into the background.

"Ruby, don't run." Twice now, a name I hadn't heard in forever had been used. Damn it, Joseph had already contacted them, the slimy little bastard. To make matters worse, they sent *him*. My stomach took a one-way trip to the bottom of my feet.

"James?"

James Wicks used to be my partner in Blue Isis. He'd been born with the ability to create and manipulate fire. I'd seen what he could do with it, and it wasn't a power I wanted to be used on myself. Taller than me, with a head of dark hair that had never been tamed.

"It's good to see you." I barely heard his soft-spoken words. "Please don't run. I don't want to hurt you." His voice sounded calm, almost reasonable and it scared the hell out of me. I didn't want to fight him, but I had no intention of going quietly. My mind went into overdrive. I needed to put some distance between us. I could use the dark to my advantage if I could reach the shelter of the trees. It would make it hard for James to focus his powers on me if he couldn't see me. Sure, he could burn down the forest. Smoke me out but that would raise too much attention. Blue Isis Operatives were all about stealth. They came in. Did the job and left without a single blade of grass out of place. They were like ninjas, except a lot deadlier. He glanced at his silent partner, and I bit back a curse. I had an unknown to deal with. Blue Isis had hired new agents. The man had a face hard to read and unknown power. He might have been human, but I wasn't going to put much faith in that being true.

My telekinesis. A raging beast when I took Joseph wasn't going to be much help. I needed to rest but I didn't think the men opposite me would wait for me to have tea and cookies.

I started to back away. "I can still beat you in a race. You've always been slow on your feet."

A heavy sigh cuts through the silence. "It's been three years. Aren't you tired of always looking over your shoulder?"

There was no doubt in my mind I would still be looking over my shoulder; I just wouldn't have anywhere to hide. "My name is Selene now."

Before I'd become a part of Blue Isis, I'd only been able to use my powers when upset. As a moody teenager, a lot of things had exploded in the house I'd shared with my foster mother. At least Blue Isis had taught me control. I pulled on my reserves. There was no way I could keep using my gifts without serious repercussions, but there wasn't an alternative. I curled my hands into fists.

"I'm not going without a fight, James. You'll need to kill me before I let you take me back. Are you ready to deliver me in a body bag?"

"Don't make me fight you, Ruby." His words were full of regret, but just because he didn't want to fight me, didn't mean he wouldn't. James was a company man. If he pushed me, he'd die one too.

I uncurled my fists. They vibrated with unleashed power, and I pushed out with my hands, hard. The air rippled like a wave until it connected with James and his silent partner. As they flew, I ran toward the darkness and made it halfway across the car park when a sharp pain ripped through my shoulder. It forced me to stumble and then hit the ground, I scraped my palms as I tried to break my fall. What the hell had just slammed into me? I scrambled to get back to my feet but hit the ground again as strong arms tackled me back down. The air whooshed from my lungs. As I struggled to turn around, I looked up into a pair of dark eyes who held my life in his hands.

James' chest pressed hard onto mine and his breath came in short bursts. I couldn't see his eyes, but he was close enough I could smell the mint toothpaste he used. My shoulder screamed in protest as I tried to fight him off, but he had me pinned to the ground, sharp stones dug into my back. A flood of memories hit me. Times like when I'd been underneath him with fewer clothes and for a whole different purpose. I pushed the thought away. It had been a lifetime ago and made the time bearable.

Pain numbed my left arm, so I pooled my power into my right. Using it at close range meant it might end up ripping a hole through the man who held me now. I kept it in check even though every part of me cried out for me to use it. "Let go of me, James," I said the words through gritted teeth. "Please."

James growled at me. "Shut up, Ruby, and hit me with a telekinetic burst. Do it quick. Frank will be back with the cuffs soon."

His words didn't make any sense. *How hard had I hit my head?* "What the hell are you going on about?" I asked, going still underneath him.

"I'm trying to save your life, dumb ass. Hit me before I change my mind." He braced himself and let go of my hand. I couldn't risk hitting him with the full blast of energy, so I pulled back on the power and aimed for a non-lethal hit. My fist connected with his shoulder and an audible pop rang out. For a brief second, I caught sight of his eyes as they widened before he flew off me and disappeared into the nearby hedges. As pain throbbed around my shoulder I scrambled back to my feet. As if the hounds of hell were biting at my heels, I vanished through a gap in the trees.

Chapter Four

I didn't know how much time had passed since I'd escaped. Reality blurred. My shoulder burned as though someone had poured lava into it. In a few hours, I'd reach the bus station in the next town. The pain in my shoulder worried the hell out of me. It wouldn't do any good if I lost consciousness in the woods. The only option was painkillers, but I couldn't risk going into town. Blue Isis was lurking in every shadow for me to slip up.

Grin and bear it, Selene. You've gotten through worse. There was the man in Rio who liked blades. The woman in London liked to put explosives on everything. I never figured out how she hooked up the shampoo bottle to explode.

Thankfully, the forest-lined the main road out of town for cover. In the end, I hadn't risked going back to the apartment, which meant all I had was the money in my back pocket, and there wasn't enough to get halfway across the state. There hadn't been time to pick up my bag when it fell from my hands. James. I couldn't linger on him and his mood which changed so fast it gave me whiplash. Luckily, I'd slipped my bank card into the inside pocket of my jacket, but only a stupid person used the one thing they could be tracked by. It would be like shooting a flare into the sky and screaming, "Hey I'm here."

I used the light from a random streetlamp to get a better look at my shoulder. Biting back a scream at the back of my throat, I moved my t-shirt aside most of my shoulder resembled a child's finger painting. Whatever Frank had done to me hadn't broken the skin but had done some serious muscle damage, even shattering the bone underneath. I gingerly moved my fingers and cried out. *Those bloody hurts.*

I took a step forward, but my feet didn't seem to want to carry me any further. I toppled over and shut my mouth before I got a mouthful of mud. I didn't bother masking my cries of pain. My whole body screamed in protest as I struggled to sit up, and half-collapsed against the trunk of a fallen tree. My eyes burned hot as tears traced wet paths down my cheeks.

I should have stayed in bed.

After taking a few deep breaths, I wiped mud out of my eyes. It took a lot of effort to shuffle out of my jacket. Freezing air brushed the bare skin of my arms and I shivered. It wouldn't be dark for long. My to-do list was stupidly long. Get out of the forest. Find somewhere safe to stay. Create a new identity. But I wouldn't accomplish any of that if I didn't get to my feet. Unfortunately, my body didn't want to listen to me. I'd used a lot of my inner reserves in the fight. My body rebelled against doing anything else. My properties shifted. I needed to rest.

I closed my eyes and listened to the natural noises of the forest. Somewhere in the undergrowth, an animal hunted for its morning meal and the birds were starting to wake up. Songs drifted to my ears and pulled me into sleep.

"HEY, CAN YOU HEAR ME?" I jerked away at the gentle pressure against my cheek. I risked opening my eyes and shut them quickly as beams of light hit them with the speed of a ten-wheeler truck. Damn, every part of me hurt. I flinched as a hand cupped my face. "You'll be all right." The voice was as calm and gentle as his hand. If he'd been surprised to find a random woman in a forest, his voice didn't show it. "Can you get to your feet?"

Now, that was an interesting question. I opened my eyes again and fought against the urge to close them. Using the tree as leverage, I tried to stand, but my legs didn't seem to want to listen. "I don't know."

"Not a problem." Strong arms found a hold under my legs and lifted me into the air. A cry escaped me as my shoulder connected with his chest.

"My name's Steven. Can you tell me yours?"

"Selene." I could have told him anything, but I'd been Selene for three years. A hard connection to break.

He stepped over something and the sound of twigs breaking under our combined weight reached my ears. Even as I curled up against him, a part of me screamed it was wrong to relax. "Can you tell me what happened?"

James' new partner hadn't even touched me, and every muscular in my shoulder feels like a dog's chew toy. Yeah, the truth didn't exactly roll off the tongue. I shook my head.

"There isn't a hospital near here. I can drive you to the nearest one. It's in the next city."

"No!" Panic swept over me. I might as well put up a neon sign that said, "Hello, escaped ex-assassin hiding here." There were too many risks. Plus, I wouldn't put it past Isis to go in all guns blazing to get me. How many people would get hurt in the process? I tried to pull away, but his hold only got tighter.

"You need to calm down or I'll end up dropping you. I can take you somewhere else it isn't close, but you can get some sleep on the backseat. It'll probably be more comfortable than where you slept last night." I don't like following orders but even if his tone was stern. There was something else in his voice. The anger drained out of me. I risked opening my eyes, his chest helped to shield my eyes from the worse of the morning sun, and glanced up. A thick head of dark hair. His eyes were a similar shade. A small smile touched his lips. I prided myself on being a good judge of character and while everything had gone to hell I still trusted that part of myself.

"Thank you."

Chapter Five

"Will she be all right?"

I rolled onto my side and peeked out under my lashes as a young voice woke me. The gaps just behind the driver's and passenger's seats were filled with bags and an ice box. I'd passed out as Stephen had laid me on the backseat and now it took some time for me to get my bearings. There was no telling how much distance we'd traveled or where we were heading.

"She'll be fine, Ethan. Whatever she's gone through was rough, but she doesn't want to go to a hospital, and I can't make her. It'll save a lot of questions." He sighed heavily. "Anyway, I've got the first aid box in the shed, and from what I can tell she isn't bleeding. It shouldn't take long to fix her up."

"Is she going to be staying?" The question was innocent enough, but it only evoked panic in the pit of my stomach. I couldn't put anyone else at risk. The Blue Isis Group had me firmly in their sights. I doubted I'd lost them for long.

"I don't know, Ethan."

When I was sure that passing out was no longer a likely outcome, I sat up. A headache blossomed behind my eyes. A groan escaped me as I rubbed the bridge of my nose. My left arm was useless; any attempt to move it sent ripples of pain through the rest of my body.

"Are you okay?"

I glanced up at the rear-view mirror and caught sight of Stephen watching me with curious eyes. Next to him in the passenger seat was a little boy. The similarities between them were impossible to miss. Dark hair and eyes. Chubbiness around his cheeks put him around six years old. The sadness in his gaze was almost tangible. What happened to someone so young for them to gain such a look? "It feels like someone hit me with a tree." I grudgingly admitted. "Where are we going?"

"Echo Falls." Stephen gestured to a road sign. "

"What's it like?" A big town meant I'd be able to hide there for a few days and rest before moving somewhere different. I needed to keep moving.

Steven frowned. "No, actually it's pretty small."

I bit my lip and glanced out of the window and at the passing scenery. Trees dotted the landscape and not much else. It was next to impossible to figure out where I was. If I didn't know where I was. It made it harder for Blue Isis to find me. "How long have I been asleep?"

"About an hour. I've got a mobile," he offered. "The reception isn't great out here, but you should be able to use it to call someone. You need to tell someone where you are?"

"No, there isn't anyone." My quick answer earned me another curious stare from the driver.

Ethan shuffled in his seat and his solemn brown eyes greeted me. I rubbed my good hand across my face and grimaced as I touched dry mud. I'd end up giving the boy nightmares. "There are some wipes in my bag." The little boy smiled shyly at me.

As I reached down for it, Ethan picked it up instead and found the baby wipes for me. The sweet gesture made me smile. "Thanks." I took the gift from him. Another half-smile crossed his face before he turned back around in his seat. As Stephen still cast curious looks my way via the rear-view mirror. I awkwardly scrubbed the rest of the mud off one-handed. Generally, I didn't like people. Only a few of them got through my defenses. Three years of freedom and I could count my friends on one hand. Hell, I could chop off four fingers and still be able to count Nikki on my thumb. There had been kids in the compound, but I didn't spend any time with them. I wanted my alone time and frankly, it freaked me out how time in the compound changed them.

They weren't kids anymore. They were monsters. Any humanity trained out of them. Ethan was the first human boy I'd seen in a long time. Stephen wasn't like the men I'd met or seen in the pub. They were both normal.

I didn't handle normal very well.

We drove in silence. Ethan hummed and Stephen tapped an uneven beat with his fingers, and I watched the scenery change dramatically, from open to lush green trees and hedges decorating the landscape. Echo Falls was a rural town. We drove past small houses, with tidy gardens to houses that would have fitted my apartment a thousand times over. After spending my life in big cities or underground compounds, I'd somehow forgotten places like this existed. I didn't like to think about my past. The life I left behind when I got recruited. I had no clue how much of it was fabricated by my stepmother. A woman who turned out to be an operative of Blue Isis. They knew about my abilities before I did and studied me. I wanted to be normal but at twelve I was anything but.

I lived in a small town like this. Meadows Alcove. I barely remembered it, but the sight of Echo Falls hit me hard. Memories just out of reach tried to grab me but I couldn't hold on to them.

As Stephen pulled into a driveway the car bounced as he drove over small stones rattling my bones. There were two stories and a large garden out the front with a tree growing in it. It wasn't as big as the other houses on the street, not by a long shot but it was still too big for just the two of them. I might not have been intending to stay for long but a quick look out of the window confirmed they had room to spare. I'd put my body through a lot, and it wouldn't have taken much to slip back into sleep. I was starting to feel as uncomfortable as hell. Places like this weren't for people like me. They were for families. Neither one of them mentioned a mom or wife, but even if they hadn't mentioned her, it didn't mean she didn't exist. Damn, she was going to get one hell of a surprise when I walked through the door with a busted shoulder and my usual wit.

As soon as the car stopped I got out of it, taking a deep breath of the clean air. I attempted a stretch and bit my lip as pain spiked through my body. James' silent partner had done a number on me. I attempted a fist, and my vision went white. That hurt. I was useless. If Blue Isis tracked me down I couldn't fight at full strength.

"You need to wait until I've had a closer look at you shoulder," Steven advised as he watched me stretch.

The man had a point and I stopped pushing myself. The only one I'd end up hurting was myself. There was every chance I'd broken it and I was screwed if I wasn't at full strength. The only thing I knew for sure was I didn't want to be stuck here. If Blue Isis found me, there was no doubt in my mind they'd hurt Steven and Ethan.

"Ethan, you better start work on your maths homework. I'll be there in a minute to help."

A smile tugged at my lips as Ethan groan in annoyance. It was obvious he was more interested in me than his schoolwork. The little boy retrieved his bag from the back seat and made his way into the house. Stephen smiled at me, an easy smile that warmed me right down to my toes. I could have blamed it on the pain, but I suddenly acutely became aware of how good-looking my rescuer was. I didn't have a type. The last relationship I was in was with James and you really couldn't call what we had a relationship. Stephen was ridiculously good-looking. Tall, with broad shoulders, and as he slipped his jacket off to reveal he wore a white t-shirt which highlighted well-defined arms. No wonder he didn't have any trouble carrying me. My rescuer kept himself in decent shape.

And I looked like absolute shit. I was covered in mud, and he was hot. I mentally slapped myself. *He's married. You can stop those naughty thoughts before they even start Selene.* It had been a long time since I'd met someone who reminded me I was a woman and the fact I hadn't had sex in three years. *And you smell Selene. You're not in any position to think of seducing him. You're on the run from a dangerous organization who wants you back. Get your hormones under control.*

"I don't usually keep supplies in the house, but there's the first aid kit in the shed. Still, there should be enough things in there to bandage your arm up." He moved my good arm over his shoulder and touched my waist. At the brief contact, any intelligent thought flew out the window. I let him guide me to the back of the house as the scent of his aftershave—dark and musky—filled my nose. *Get a grip, Selene, you haven't been ruled by your body's insane reactions before and he certainly isn't the only hot guy you know.* I wasn't interested in adding complications to my ever-growing list. The problem was if I kept breathing in his aftershave all bets were off.

"Can you tell me how it happened?"

"I slipped." I'd spent the last three years as a different person. If lying was an Olympic sport, I would get a gold medal. "I tripped over a fallen branch and hit my shoulder on a tree. I shouldn't have been hiking in the woods alone." His body tensed. "I appreciate the help. It would have taken days for anyone to find me." I could feel the pause as if he was about to say something.

In the end, he coughed. "You might want to hold thanking me until I reset your arm. It'll hurt, a lot."

"You have got experiences in setting arms, right?"

A smile tugged at the corner of his mouth. "It's been a few years, but I still think I remember the basics of it." That didn't fill me with confidence, but I didn't have a better option. Stephen caught the expression on my face. "I've trained to be a doctor, but I didn't take my final tests. Selene, you're safe. I wouldn't do it if I thought I might end up hurting you worse."

He moved my arm about with practiced ease. I focussed on the feel of his hand and fingers on my skin and did my best to ignore the stabs of pain. "What does your wife have to say about your habit of rescuing strays?" The wife hadn't made an appearance yet, which was odd.

His body tensed again. "Georgina isn't with us anymore. She died after Ethan was born."

"I'm sorry," I mumbled. Crap, he was single? I didn't want to hear that. Sure, I found him attractive, and he would make a great distraction, but I knew it was a bad idea. Unfortunately, my libido wasn't interested in common sense.

He glanced toward the house, not meeting my eyes. Was it the reason Ethan looked sad and lost? "Don't be. It happened a long time ago."

"So, it's the two of you in such a big house?"

Steven nodded. "I need to let you go so I can unlock the door. Can you keep your balance?" He changed the subject quickly, but I still noticed. He didn't want to talk about the dead wife, and I didn't want to either. It wasn't any of my business and I didn't plan on staying long enough for it to become my business. I reached out, using the wooden wall to keep upright

"I'm okay, not a problem."

Steven retrieved a small ring of keys from out of his pocket and searched through them. When the door was finally opened he put his arm back around my waist. "Do you have anywhere to go?"

"Not anymore," I confessed. "But I'll be fine," I added quickly. I didn't want anyone to feel sorry for me. I might not have chosen this life, but it was still mine and I managed to look after myself quite well. For the most part. There was a small round table, two chairs, and worktables attached to the wall. There was one large red toolbox and several cupboard boxes. I spied the first aid kit he'd left on one of the worktops. He kept the area clean from rubbish, but it looked like the space was used for storage rather than actual work.

I moved away from the support of his arm and hobbled over to the table and the available seat. He pulled the other one closer and sat down. "I need to remove your jacket. I need to get a better look at your shoulder."

With my teeth gritted, Steven helped me take off my jacket. Pain shot through me before it settled into a red-hot pulse that shot down my arm and across my collarbone. I squeezed my eyes shut until he stopped moving my shoulder. A small cry of pain escaped my lips. I'd gone through training to deal with damage to my body, to push it to the back of my mind. I guess the lesson hadn't stuck.

"What hit you?"

I focussed on his voice, the way it traveled over my skin. It robbed the pain of its harshness. "I said, I tripped and fell into a tree."

"It must have been one hell of a tree." His fingers were gentle as he moved the neckline of my shirt aside. Curiosity made me want to take a better look as well. Steven's hand on my chin guided my gaze up and into his. My breath caught in my throat as I was transfixed by how close we were. The last person to be this close had been Joseph and the look in his eyes had been anything but sweet. Stephen had nothing to gain from helping me. There hadn't been enough people in the world who wanted to be sweet or kind to me, without a motive. I bit my bottom lip and pulled away from his touch.

Steven coughed. I wasn't the only one confused by the tension between us. "It'll be better if you don't see it. Whatever happened to you, it looks like your shoulder's dislocated. Can you wriggle your fingers for me?"

I did as he asked and bit back another cry of pain. "How long until I get the feeling back?" A shiver went through me that had nothing to do with how much it hurt as Steven studied my shoulder more closely. His dark hair tickled my nose and I fought against the urge to breathe in deeply. Damn, this was embarrassing. I looked like shit and my hormones were raging out of control.

"A few weeks maybe more if you're not careful with it." He took a deep breath. "I need to pop it back into place. This is going to hurt."

"Just do it." I used my bad arm to hold onto his shoulder, with my gaze locked on his. *It's going to be too easy to get lost in the pain.* If I started screaming I didn't think I'd be able to stop again. Steven moved off his seat and position himself in front of me. He pushed against me, a hard jolt and a scream ripped through me, and the table collapsed.

Steven jumped away in surprise. "What the hell?"

I'd gained a great deal of control over my telekinetic gifts, but bursts of emotions sometimes resulted in something breaking. "Was that an old table?" Pools of tears had gathered in the corner of my eyes, but the sharp pain didn't stop me from trying to make light of the situation. The chance he might link my yelp of pain to the now broken table was non-existent but still, I went into deflect mode. I blinked the moisture out of my eyes and hot tears rolled down my cheeks. *Ouch..*

Steven shook his head. "No, it's new." He glanced back at me and noticed my obvious pain for the first time. "You okay? I'm sorry this isn't going to get any better until I bandaged it up." For the next few minutes, he wrapped my arm. Pulling it gently across my body, he used the bandages to attach it securely to my chest. My hand ended up resting on my shoulder. "You need to keep this as dry as possible. Do you need a hand getting clean?"

For a second I forgot how to breathe as scenarios raced through my head which ended up with both of us getting wet. It looked like I wasn't going to be able to control how my body reacted to him. I pushed the thoughts to the back of my mind and into the pile of mentally marked, things to contemplate later. He had a son. The thought of his son made an effective splash of cold hard reality. I had a crazed group hot on my tail. It had bad timing written all over it. "Do you have a shower?"

He double-checked the bandage. "Yeah, that's probably a better idea."

"Oh, I don't know, maybe if the situation was better, I wouldn't mind you helping me in the shower." I smiled as Steven's eyes widened in surprise. The words slipped out of my mouth without a second thought.

Chapter Six

I kept my back to the warm spray. The mud swirled down the plughole and vanished but my presence in the shower left a mark. Purple bruises decorated my skin even if they didn't hurt now. I'd feel every one of them in the morning. My body was going to hurt in the worst way after a good night's sleep. I turned the water off then stepped out from underneath the shower and nudged the door open with my hip. Cool air blasted me, and I shivered.

I plucked a towel from its resting place on the back of the door and bit my lip as I tried to fasten it around my chest. I brushed my free hand across the mirror and peered into it. My reflection stared back at me. The worse of the damage was hidden by the bandage but tinier bruises dotted my chest. I'd been in worse situations, for the life of me none of them came to mind. I was in a house of strangers. It went against every instinct that Blue Isis had drilled into me. Never trust strangers. The only people you could trust were the Collective and in truth, you couldn't trust those sneaky bastards at all. I glanced towards the door. The sounds of a happy family. A small child and a man, they weren't dangerous. Neither of them could hurt me. So why would they scare me?

"Are you okay in there?"

I twisted awkwardly; Steven's voice had taken me completely by surprise. A surge of power swept over me, and a few bottles fell out of the cabinet. It could have been worse, but my power reserves were running on empty, and the outburst left me even more tired. I hadn't even heard Steven walk upstairs. I needed food and a bed before I started to feel anything close to genetically engineered human. "I'm fine."

"Selene?"

He sounded concerned. I wasn't used to people caring about me. It made me uncomfortable. Ties made you weak. It gave Blue Isis something to use against you. "I'm fine." The words left me in close to a growl.

"I'm leaving you some clothes in front of the door. I'm not sure if they'll fit you, but they're better than nothing. There's a toothbrush on top of them. If you're hungry I've made something to eat."

I moved to the door, closed my eyes, and rested my head against the wooden panel. There wasn't any point in being a bitch. Steven hadn't needed to help me. Without him, I would still be wandering the woods, already in Blue Isis's clutches. James helped me to escape once but I doubt I'd get that lucky again. "I'm sorry. It's been a rough day and I shouldn't take it out on you."

"Don't worry about it. We'll meet you downstairs." I listened as he made his way away from the door. When I was sure Steven was gone, I opened the door far enough to awkwardly gather up the clothes one-handed and noticed the toothbrush which Steven left on the top. I cleaned my teeth first before searching through the clothes. Steven had covered all the bases. The kind gesture made me smile as I slipped on a pair of jeans. They didn't fit well around my waist but at least the legs were the right length. Since I'd ended up cutting my bra and t-shirt off, I picked up a white vest and wrestled it on. I wriggled and huffed as I pulled it down. A little tight across the chest but it was better than nothing.

I carefully brushed the knots out of my hair and then pulled the strands over my shoulder. My movements were clumsy and uncoordinated. A job that should have taken five minutes took twenty instead. By the time I was finished I was hot, uncomfortable, and annoyed.

But at least I was dressed.

The whole situation was completely alien to me. My parents had died when I was four. I didn't have any clear memories of them when I was adopted by Lily. Well, it wasn't the most nurturing environment, to begin with, and it got worse when I found out the truth. Lily had shown me how to use my telekinesis. How to focus on one object without it raging out of control. At the time I hadn't known she'd been working for Blue Isis. Then, as soon as I hit eighteen, she handed me off to be trained as a killer. Not all of us weren't killers. Some were spies. Others were soldiers. None of us truly had a choice.

I glanced at my reflection. It was an unspoken rule of mine that I never thought of Lily. The woman hadn't been a part of my life for a long time. She didn't deserve my thoughts. The woman had made my childhood non-existent. I'd been an assignment. A tool. A freak. I shook my head. I had more important things to worry about I was living on borrowed time. If Blue Isis had been able to find me in a dead-end town under an assumed name, they could find me anywhere.

I leaned against the sink and frowned at my reflection.

"Get it together, Selene."

THE SMELL OF GARLIC weaved upstairs, and my stomach growled at me, loud enough that it was a little embarrassing. I hadn't eaten for twenty-four hours, and my body had no intention of letting me forget it.

The house looked more like a home than the apartment I left behind. The place had wooden floorboards everywhere, a rug thrown here and there, which was a burst of color that made it feel less cold. There were photographs on the walls—Ethan at school, playing football, and hiking in the hills. I assumed that Steven was the one who had taken them. There weren't any pictures of Georgina. He must have kept them in a photo album somewhere. I was a lot more curious than I wanted to admit. Steven had been elusive and that was why he piqued my curiosity.

I passed a living room. There were toys pushed into a corner, and the television screen was black. I made my way to where I thought the kitchen might be. Ethan was already sitting at the table with a book open in front of him. Steven had changed into a pair of well-worn jeans and a clean blue shirt. I shifted my gaze down the curve of his back before I even realized what I was doing.

"I wasn't sure what you'd like, so I kept it simple." There was an obvious tension in the way he held his body; I wasn't the only one nervous about the situation.

I glanced at the counter in surprise. Cut up fruit in bowls, buttered bread, vegetables, and Spaghetti Bolognese. I breathed in deeply as my mouth started to water. "It smells great."

Steven smiled. "Thanks, it's one of Ethan's favorites. Take a seat and I'll get the plates. It's time to put your things away kiddo."

Ethan collected up his books and hopped off his chair. He smiled at me, shyly before he disappeared from the room. After a few seconds, he rushed back in and hopped back onto his chair.

It was a beautiful kitchen. A long breakfast table played host to most of the food which certainly didn't come out of a box like most of my food did. Black and purple tiles covered the walls above the oven, sink, and work surfaces. Wooden slates covered the floor and a round table was pushed against the wall. Only three of the four chairs were accessible. I hadn't seen anything like that outside of a magazine. The apartment I lived in with Nikki had been basic, with none of the homelier touches. There hadn't been any money to make it look like a home. Would my life be like this if I hadn't been born gifted if my parents hadn't died? What kind of person would I be if I hadn't learned how to kill someone at a hundred paces with a well-placed thought?

I've never entertained the thought of having kids, working as an assassin wasn't the most stable environment for raising a family. Never had a boyfriend, unless you counted James, but that was more an enjoyable version of stress relief than any real connection. The world I came from wasn't meant for children and I doubted Blue Isis believed in maternity pay.

The youngest Blue Isis ever recruited had been fourteen. Her screams had brought me out of my room. She'd fought against them until the Leech joined them in the hallway. The girl had been incredibly strong, shrugging the men off as if they weighed nothing. The man with the white eyes had changed all that; leeches could siphon off a person's gift as if they'd never had it.

Steven wiped his hands on a kitchen towel. "He's special, intelligent too. Must have gotten it from his mum." There was no way she could miss the pride in his eyes or the smile on his face. Ethan glanced up from his chair as Steven placed the plates down. "I hope you're both hungry."

DINNER WAS EXHAUSTING. Steven kept trying to pry information out of me. I did my best to swerve the conversation to other topics. It was an odd game of misdirection, but it was one I had down to a fine art. As soon as he finished his food, Ethan asked to be excused, and from the sudden burst of sound from somewhere in the house, I knew he'd switched on the TV. I helped to collect the plates and stacked them near the sink. After three platefuls of food, my stomach had stopped grumbling. I glanced out of the window. It was beautiful here in the middle of nowhere. The sun made everything seem brighter, more vibrant. A part of me wanted to stay, but Blue Isis knew I was on the run. I lived on borrowed time, and I didn't want them to get hurt because of who I was. After a while, Ethan had started to relax around me and the thought of anything happening to him or his father tore me up inside.

"I need to go. Where's the nearest bus station?"

As I'd been having my mini pep talk, Steven had still been at the table, a cup of coffee in front of him. Mine was near the kettle and I picked it up, breathing in the heady aroma before sipping it. A girl could seriously get used to having good coffee on tap and a beautiful view. I glanced over my shoulder, and I wasn't just talking about the garden. There was something about him, both, which called to me—a part of me I thought never existed to start with. He leaned in his chair; his long legs crossed at the ankle with his cup in his hand resting against his flat stomach. "You can't travel in your condition."

"I've just hurt my shoulder. It's not like I'm pregnant or something." I carefully wriggled my shoulder. It still felt like someone stamped on it, but thanks to the bandages it didn't hurt as much. "I don't have anywhere else to go, but it's best if I keep moving."

As he sighed I turned around resting against the counter. "If you told me what you were running from I might be able to help."

"That's sweet and I don't get me wrong, I appreciate all the help you've given me already, but I don't owe you answers." It came out harsh, but deep down I knew the only person I could trust was myself. If I got emotionally attached to either of them I'd slip up and make a mistake.

Steven raised his hands like he was approaching a wounded animal. Couldn't blame him for that, I felt like one. "Take it as advice from your doctor. You need to rest that shoulder or you're at risk of making it worse. Do you want that?" He folded his arms across his chest, and he had a no-nonsense look about him.

He had a point. "No, of course, I don't."

"Then it's settled. You can stay here until that shoulder of yours starts to feel better."

My mouth opened in surprise. Was Steven offering me a place to stay? "You don't even know me, and you want me to stay with you and your son?"

Steven got to his feet and started to clear away the rest of the plates. He didn't look at me as he worked, but it wasn't easy to take my eyes off him. He's an actual nice guy. Hard to believe they existed anymore. Not once since he'd patched up my shoulder had he peeked at my chest or made me feel uncomfortable. The ability to read someone was the first lesson I'd learned with Blue Isis. It's how I'd figured out Joseph had been a slime-ball even before he'd tried to rape me in his office.

"Look, if you're worried about staying in a strange house, I understand that. I can set up a bed in the shed. You've already been in there. So, you know there's plenty of space. There's also a heater in there, so you won't get cold."

I knew that I shouldn't say yes, however tempting the thought was. These guys were normal. They shouldn't be infected by my world. Steven must have seen that my resolve was breaking because he pressed on. He took small steps until he was finally in front of me. I glanced down as he briefly touched my elbow before looking back up and into his eyes. "I can understand the need to run away from your problems, whatever they are they'll catch up with you sooner rather than later. In your current state, you won't be a match for them."

I should say no, but he had a point, one that I hated to admit was right. "I'll stay for a few days."

As if he only just noticed the closeness between us, he stepped away. "I'll sort out the bedding. Why don't you sit in the living room with Ethan? I'll tell you when it's done."

THE LAST FEW HOURS had been surreal, then everything about the day had been the same. I'd eventually excused myself when Steven took his son up to bed. I didn't know how I felt about the man who'd saved me, but the more distance between us the better. There were fewer chances of me doing something I wouldn't be able to take back, like kissing him which was tempting. I groaned as I rolled onto my back, being careful not to knock my shoulder. The professional detachment had been a class Blue Isis had taught. It made it easier to get yourself close enough to a target without anyone suspecting you were there to kill them. Unfortunately, it looked like my skills were a little rusty. It was everything in the house. It reminded me of the life Blue Isis took away from me. I didn't want to admit I missed it, being normal. Even if I hadn't been that way for long.

My mind refused to shut down. All those years of not dwelling on the past and now it was all I could think about. How much had the place changed? The teams back then had been tight, usually, two manned with a third in the background. In hostile areas, the third was usually me perched on a rooftop with a sniper rifle. With the added telekinesis, it meant I never missed a shot. Why did they want me back? I'd burnt a lot of bridges to get out of that place and I'd rather die than go back to it.

The night passed by slowly and while I was sure I didn't sleep properly, I still managed to doze. My shoulder made it impossible to rest, but it was nothing a couple of cups of coffee wouldn't cure and a nap in the afternoon. As soon as the sun started to come through the windows, I swung my legs over the side of the cot and stood. I carefully stretched out; the t-shirt Steven had given me brushed against the top of my thighs. My shoulder was back to a dull throbbing pain instead of screaming agony which was certainly a blessing. As soon as I pulled the t-shirt off, goose bumps erupted all over my skin. I quickly dressed and brushed out my hair with my fingers. It took a while before the coldness which had seeped into my bones vanished.

With invisible fingers, I brushed against my telekinesis like it was a well-loved pet hidden underneath my skin. It was reckless to use my gifts so close to strangers, but it was still early enough in the day everyone should still be asleep. I was at a disadvantage having one arm. The only time I'd recently used my telekinesis had been in extreme circumstances. I needed to fine-tune it, for it to answer me without pain or anger guiding it.

I reached out and drew on the power like unraveling a ball of string. The boots shook like a mini earthquake came to life beneath them before they flew straight through the air. I yelped as they hit my ankles. Next time I needed to practice with more space. I rubbed my ankles. Ouch. I glanced between my boots and my naked feet, then to my bandaged arm.

"How am I going to manage this?"

Chapter Seven

The backdoor was unlocked. I closed my eyes and strained my ears. After a few seconds, I concluded the house was empty. Steven and Ethan had left to go somewhere. The trust in that guy was amazing and a little stupid. What kind of person left their house unattended with the back door open? If I hadn't felt comfortable before about being in the house, I certainly wasn't now. There wouldn't be much warning if people rushed in with guns. My stomach growled at me, but I knew the chances Blue Isis found me here were slim to none and headed to the kitchen. I eyed the cereal box left on the table and went in search of a bowl. As I went to retrieve milk, I noticed the note on the fridge.

"Morning Selene. I needed to drop Ethan off at school. I'll be back soon. Please help yourself to anything you want in the fridge. Steven."

I left the note on the fridge door, got milk and orange juice out then closed it again. After I'd found a glass, I made myself a drink. As soon as I was finished I tidied my things away.

Steven hadn't said what he did for a living, but he had to do something to keep a house like this. There was a box of cleaning things by the back door. The smell of cleaning fluid in the air. Did he hire someone? I didn't like the idea someone else had been in the house cleaning and I hadn't been any the wiser.

I frowned. There wasn't much I could do about it now and whoever it had been hadn't come to the shed. I needed to find a map and figure out where the hell I was. There had been plenty of places I'd seen because of Blue Isis, but I hadn't made many trips to the smaller cities in the middle of nowhere. How much distance was between me and the life I'd left behind at the Golden Eagle?

I switched on the kettle and then explored the bottom floor of the house. It was obvious that a child lived there. There were toys in the living room, most of them were in a wooden chest but some were still on the floor. My foot knocked against a red truck, and I scooped down to pick it up. The walls were painted beige with paintings and photographs pinned up. I put the truck down with the other toys and studied the photographs. There were several of Ethan through all stages of his life. The solemn look was in each one even if a smile curved his lips. There were a few of Ethan and Steven. Who had taken those? I gradually stopped in front of a fireplace and picked the photograph off the mantle.

The woman in them wore a graduation cap and robe, her blonde hair was pinned up and kept underneath the cap. She was pretty, smiling, and at ease. Georgina.

I put the photograph down feeling like I was intruding. The furniture was nice if a little mismatched like he'd bought them at a thrift store, or they'd been donated. The bookcase in the corner was filled with paperbacks, mostly about crime. Judging from the titles the top shelves were Steven's. The slightly brighter covers on the bottom shelves belonged to Ethan.

It was only when I was in the hallway that I noticed the small table. There was an old-school telephone with a circular dial. Underneath it, Steven kept some papers and two books. I left my cup on the table and knelt to get a closer look at the books. The smaller one was a map and I flicked through it. Echo Falls was small as Steven said it was. The town itself was surrounded by trees and there were hiking paths highlighted through the woods. I scanned the page a few more times until I find what I'd been searching for—a teeny tiny icon that stood for a public telephone on the outskirts of town. I took the map with me into the kitchen. I wasn't planning on leaving today, but it would make sense to study it for an escape route out of town in case I needed to leave in a hurry.

There was no telling how long my luck was going to last. The thought made my stomach twist in knots. I had to be out of there before they figured out where I was.

"I'M HOME," STEVEN CALLED out as soon as the front door was open. A shiver of excitement shot up my spine. Although it was tempting to get to know him better. I had more important things on my mind than seducing him. There was a grunt and a thud as shoes hit the wall. "Selene, are you in here?"

"In the kitchen."

I glanced up from studying the map as he appeared in the doorway. My reaction to the sight of him in a pair of worn jeans and a blue sweater was ridiculous. My heart skipped a beat, my mouth went dry, and all coherent thought took a flying leap out the window with my common sense. His dark hair had been brushed away from his forehead and it drew my attention to his eyes and the slightly bemused expression in them. My face went hot, and I turned my attention to the map in front of me breaking eye contact with him. All the feelings that welled up inside of me to were pushed to the back of my mind. This was why I preferred to be alone. It was impossible to form attachment when you only had yourself for company. It had been a long time since I'd trusted someone enough to spend time with them. Three years without a relationship or anyone to help me scratch an itch. At the time, the only reason I'd moved in with Nicki was that Blue Isis would have been searching for a girl living by herself. I never thought Nicki would become my first friend, A normal human girl who worked too much and hated her job. In the end, I'd left her without a backward glance, like I how I would need to leave Ethan and Steven eventually.

Alone again. I tried to ignore the pang in my chest.

"Morning. How's the shoulder?" He walked past me and toward the kettle. "Do you want another coffee?"

I nodded and smiled. "It's feeling a lot better." A blatant lie, but one I told for the greater good. I needed to get out of the house. The only way either of them would be safe was if I was in another state. It had been years since I'd even been tempted to get involved with anyone. This wasn't the right time or the right situation. It never would be. How well had it ended with James? He'd tried to take me back to the group I didn't want to be in.

As I took one last look at the map, Steven made both of us a cup of coffee. "It's only been a day, Selene. Unless you heal superhuman fast, it'll still feel tight where the muscles seize up. Am I right?"

I reached up with my free hand and rubbed my shoulder a little. My teeth gritted in reflex. Steven was by my side, holding my hand, making the movement softer, gentler. "You have to be careful when you touch it," he said concerned. "The muscles need time to heal."

"You keep saying that."

"Maybe you should start listening to me then?"

What had I said about keeping a professional distance from him? The room immediately felt too small, and my hand burned from the simple touch. He hadn't noticed. Instead, he gently rubbed my shoulder until a spark of pleasure took over from the pain. As his fingers moved up and down the curve of my neck, my head dropped forward, and I closed my eyes as a moan escaped me. I snapped my eyes open again. Had that noise come from me?

Steven stopped and I glanced over my shoulder. The tension was back, but now it was different, supercharged. His eyes were now completely black. I hadn't been the only one who enjoyed it. He dropped his hand. Need rose inside of me. My emotions, usually held under tight control, were rebelling in a big way. I broke eye contact and I stood, I needed to get out of the house. Some fresh air would help clear my head.

The decision was taken out of my hands as Steven darted around me touched my waist and pulled me against him. "This is insane." Those words were the only thing I heard before he kissed me. All the tension left me as he gave a soft and tender kiss as if he was scared he'd hurt me. With my free hand, I touched his chest and put the slightest pressure on it. Steven broke the contact, every breath tight and controlled. "I didn't mean for that to happen."

"That's my line." I curled my fingers into the front of his sweater. I fought a war with myself, a part of me wanted to push him away. The other wanted to see if the kitchen table was as sturdy as it looked. "I'm not staying, Steven. I'm here until my shoulder heals and then I'm gone. Do you want to get involved with a woman like me?" Would he accept me as a telekinetic assassin? Would anyone?

He brushed a kiss against my forehead, the move sweet and unexpected. "I haven't been able to stop thinking about you."

"I mean you found me unconscious in the woods. Can't get any more mysterious than that." The corner of my lips kicked up into a small smile as I pulled away from him, releasing his shirt. "I'm going to go for a walk." The more distance between us the better. I might have been aiming for professional, but I wasn't a saint by any stretch of the imagination. Any more incentive and I'd be doing several things I'd regret in the morning.

"Where are you going?" His voice was husky and sexy as hell.

"I've spent most of the morning studying the map of the area. It's time I went and explored." I might have needed to make that phone call, but I wasn't going to risk using their phone. There was no telling if Nicki's phone would be tapped, and I didn't want to bring the group to the small town. What was the situation back at the Golden Eagle? Had James and his partner questioned the people there?

"Do you want some company?"

"I'll be okay. How much trouble can I get into in a town this small anyway?"

SINCE I'D THOUGHT OF an escape route in case I needed to leave in a hurry, I decided to stop at the information center in the middle of the village. I hadn't been able to get the kiss out of my mind. It flew around like a ping pong ball. There were moments in your life you couldn't take back. That wasn't one of them. Okay, I knew it was a bad idea, but the way he'd kissed me? It was seared onto my memory; I wouldn't be forgetting it anytime soon.

Instead, I focussed on Echo Falls. It was one thing to look at it on a map and quite another to see it up close and personal. When Steven had driven into town, I'd been out of it, only taking in the things it was hard to miss. Now, I caught tiny details. The gardens were extremely well kept. Some old people sat on porches and there were young children in the gardens. After spending my life in foreign countries and the dead-end town which had been home to the Golden Eagle, this place was perfect. I didn't have any reason not to, but I didn't trust it.

The information center turned out to be a small wooden building with windows that looked too big for it. Cool air-conditioned air hit me as I walked into the bright room. A tiny woman manned the desk. Dwarfed by the large counter, a tiny woman with short white hair cut and with oversized glasses perched on her nose, made her resemble a startled owl. She glanced up as soon as I walked in.

"Good afternoon Welcome to Echo Falls." The smile she flashes at me is infectious and I smile. I'd gone through my life with a scowl on my face that made most people give me a wide berth. I was the girl you didn't want to meet down a dark alley and it was a reputation that I worked hard on. Blue Isis was a place of monsters. Monsters with human faces. I didn't trust people. They weren't worth it. The operatives at Blue Isis were all out for themselves. You slipped up and they'd ship you off to see the people in charge, for re-education.

In the space of two days, I'd met three people who made me smile, and it didn't feel forced. My reputation was going to be ruined if this ever got out. Selene, the killer. So cold you never saw her smile.

"Afternoon."

She frowned as she studied me. "Are you here for the hiking? I've got some brilliant books on the local wildlife and the trails."

A wild guess A bad one since I didn't even vaguely look like a hiker. I shook my head. "I'm just visiting."

She pushed her glasses, which had slid to the tip of her nose, back up again. "Where are you staying?"

Since I'd spent the last three years evading questions, I was tempted not to say anything. It wasn't any of her business. On the other hand, I was also sure if Blue Isis managed to track me now, they wouldn't be using little Red Riding Hood's grandmother to trap me. "I'm staying with Steven and Ethan."

The old woman frowned. "They didn't say that they had company staying over." She looked perplexed.

"Why would they?"

"I was there this morning cleaning up before Ethan went to school. Steven didn't mention you," the older woman commented as she shuffled through the books in front of her.

Why would he mention me? Had he finally figured out I didn't want people knowing where I was? "I don't know why he didn't mention me, but I'm staying there for a few days."

The frown quickly vanished replaced with the smile from earlier. "Any friend of the boys is a friend of mine. What can I help you with?"

I glanced around the room, but I couldn't see anything I needed. "A bus timetable and a more detailed map of the area would be great, thanks."

Her smile brightens. "I'll be right back."

Chapter Eight

The little old lady handed me some pamphlets and pointed me in the direction of the nearest telephone box. Calling home wasn't my best idea, but the way my week was shaping up it wasn't the worse. After I found out Nicki was okay I would never call her again. My tie to her would need to be cut. I tried to ignore the pang of regret. We'd spent a lot of time together. Walking home in the middle of the night, having coffee and a chat before we went to bed.

"Hello?" Nicki's slightly tired voice made me smile.

I took a deep breath and sighed. "Hey Nicki, it's Selene."

"Where the hell are you? I've been worried sick." Surprise quickly turned to anger with a speed that would have given me whiplash.

"I'm in the middle of nowhere." I didn't go into too much detail. If the phone was tapped, I couldn't risk it. I didn't have much time. They could track me that way. "How's everything at work. Any strange people turn up asking questions?"

For a second she doesn't say anything. I think she's shocked judging from the all-encompassing silence on the other side of the phone. It took her a while to get over it. "You've been missing for days, Selene, and the first question you have is about the job you hate?"

"It's important, Nicki."

"Work is work." She snapped. "When are you coming back?"

"I'm not."

"What do you mean you're not coming back?" She shrieked and I held the handset away from my ear. Yikes. "I need you here. I'm sorry if this sounds selfish, but how am I supposed to pay for the flat? Joseph is being more of an asshole than usual. I don't know if he'll give me any more shifts to cover it."

Finally, what I needed to hear about. "So, Joseph is still around?"

Nicki scoffed as if I'd asked a stupid question. "Of course, he's still here. Joseph is as old as the furniture. He'll never leave. He's incredibly angry with you for not turning up for your shifts. What the hell happened between the two of you?"

"He nearly raped me." I didn't mention I kicked his ass. "That's why I can't come back. Nicki, you need to get out of there."

There was another shocked-filled silence, but Nicki knew how Joseph was. The slimy excuse for a man thought he could get away with anything. How many other girls he'd tried to force himself on? Or had I been the only one since he had something against me? "Oh my god, Selene. Are you okay?"

"I'm fine. Listen to me. I need you to go into my room and have a look at my fireplace. There's a loose brick on, the left-hand side, the eighth brick up. Behind it, there's a small box, I want you to take the money and I want you to leave town. I can't explain, but there's enough money in there for you to start somewhere new."

"Selene, you're scaring me." I could hear it in her voice. For all her bravado, Nicki knew the world was dangerous. Staying at the Golden Eagle was a bad idea. I couldn't risk Joseph going after her because he didn't have two brain cells to rub together, and he thought revenge would bring me back.

I took a deep breath. "I need you to trust me, Nicki. You need to pack a bag, take the money, and leave tonight. Use the money to travel. Don't use any cards as they'll be easy to trace."

"Can you at least tell me where you are? Can I come to you?"

"It wouldn't be a clever idea." There wasn't any point in telling her the phones might be bugged. It would only scare her. "I'm glad to hear you're okay. Goodbye, Nicki."

Her breath caught as my words sank in. We wouldn't be seeing each other again. "Goodbye, Selene."

"WE'VE GOT TO GO TO a dentist appointment after I pick up Ethan. Will you be all right alone for a few hours?"

I hadn't been back for long. Both of us hadn't mentioned the kiss, but it had been all I could think about as I walked through the door and laid eyes on him. The tension was unbearable, and it was only getting worse. "I'll be fine." I smiled at him over the book I'd borrowed from his shelf.

"We'll bring back some food, so don't worry about cooking anything." He lingered in the doorway for a second. "We can talk later, about the kiss? I don't want you to feel uncomfortable about staying with us."

I closed the book, running my hands over the smooth cover. "Okay, we'll talk later." There wasn't a promise of us continuing what we started, but I let my gaze drift back to his lips. I guess my body had different ideas.

IT WAS DARK OUTSIDE when I heard a knock on the front door. I closed the book as the hairs on the back of my neck stood on end. Steven hadn't mentioned anyone coming. I pulled the knife I'd stashed underneath the cushion free. Hiding it behind my back I made my way to the front door. It was dark outside, and I couldn't get a good look at the shadow on the other side of the door. Had they found me? How? I took a deep breath and let it out. The tension in my body goes with it. I had to be sure. Couldn't get stab happy on someone paying a visit. It would be hard to explain away a dead body. I opened the door and sighed. *Oh crap, I should have ignored it.* "I'm sorry we're not buying what you're selling." As I closed the door, the man stuck his foot out. The light from the hallway caught the smoothness of his head. The Blue Isis needed to change their uniform, everything about them screamed, "I'm a secret agent." The black suit was expensive, and I couldn't even see where the gun was.

"Hello, Ms. Williams."

My knuckles hurt due to a grip I couldn't break on the door. I didn't bother to deny it. They knew who I was. "What do you want?" The knife was heavy in my hand. If I stabbed him I would need to clean up the blood. Did I have enough time before Steve and Ethan got back? It had already been a couple of hours. They could be here any minute.

"Isn't it obvious? We want you." He didn't bother to try to force his way into the house. He just stood there as if he had all the time in the world. "It's time to come back home."

"It's never been my home."

He smirked. "Either way, it's time to come back."

I pooled my telekinesis into my fist with the knife in it. If he tried to grab me, I'd hit him so hard his teeth would rattle. "It's not my life anymore. It's time for you to leave, or I'll make you."

He clenched his hand into a fist and the air around me went cold. "Do you think they would have sent someone without a gift? I'll make this easy for you. I'll even give you time to say goodbye to Steven and Ethan." He must have read the surprise in my eyes. "Yes, I know their names."

"And if I don't come with you?"

"Then I'm going to get better acquainted with your new friends." The way he said it he could have been talking about the weather. The coldness behind his eyes told me all I needed to know. I just didn't want to believe it.

"You wouldn't hurt Ethan, he's just a kid." Blue Isis made monsters, but a six-year-old boy? They had to draw a line somewhere, didn't they? Doubt hit me.

"I wouldn't get any enjoyment out of it, but it would be your fault not mine because you didn't come with me when I offered you the chance."

Chapter Nine

I was sitting in the kitchen when Ethan and Steven returned. The old me would have already been halfway across the state, not caring I put them in harm's way. Fortunately, I wasn't her anymore. I should have realized that I started to get emotionally attached to them. It didn't help me now. The only way to keep them safe would be to leave tonight with the man who hadn't even bothered to give me his name.

"Selene!" Ethan exclaimed happily. "Daddy said since I don't need any fillings I could have ice cream. Do you want some?"

The eager smile on his face coaxed one out of me. I glanced up at the clock. There was still time. One more normal memory before everything changed. Anger swelled to life inside of me, but I smiled. "I'll get the bowls."

Ethan had already disappeared into the hallway to put his coat away as Steven closed the door behind them. It was then I noticed it was raining outside. His dark hair was damp, curling at the sides. He shook his head and water droplets hit me. We were supposed to talk about the kiss tonight, but I planned on leaving before we had the chance. Call me a coward but drawing the moment out was just too hard. Distracted by a stray raindrop as it worked its way down the front of his shirt, I hadn't realized he watched me.

"Are you okay?"

"I'm fine." It hadn't been hard to come to the decision I wouldn't be telling him what was happening. Steven was the kind of guy who wanted to rescue people. An old-fashioned knight-in-shining-armor but I'd never needed a knight to rescue me before. I couldn't risk anything happening to him and leaving Ethan without another parent.

I used to be a highly trained assassin. It was time to deal with this, even if I didn't walk away from it.

"Selene?" He took a step toward me. He gently placed his hands on my shoulders. I glanced up and into his brown eyes. "You can talk to me. Whatever you're going through, I can help."

If I got onto my tiptoes I'd be able to close the distance between us. I couldn't drag my gaze off his lips. I looked up. His gaze had drifted down to my mouth. He lowered his head and while there was nothing I wanted more, I put my hand on his chest, stopping him.

"Let's go get some ice cream."

I COULDN'T KEEP MY eyes from looking at the clock. Nervous energy filled every part of me. I bounced my spoon off the table. It made a dull thudding sound as it connected with the solid surface. I glanced up to see they were studying me. I put the spoon back down on the table and tapped my foot instead.

"It's time to say goodnight to Selene and head upstairs to brush your teeth. I'll be up in a minute."

Ethan shuffled out of his chair and with a speed fuelled by chocolate ice cream, kissed me on the cheek then rushed out of the kitchen before I'd even registered it. I quickly got to my feet, collected the empty bowls, and took them to the sink. I should have been more careful. Neither of them would understand why I left. Steven might blame himself because of the kiss the only upside was Ethan was young, he'd forget about me as if I'd never existed.

As I turned around, he was there. The memory of the kiss came back to haunt me. It had taken a lot of self-control to not close the gap between us. His hands were on my shoulders and all it would take for him to let me go was for me to say no. I didn't want to say no. I threw my arms around his neck, forgetting the pain in my shoulder, and crashed my lips against his. There was no finesse in it, but, his arms went around my waist, and I was pulled tight against him, he didn't want finesse.

And neither did I.

A moan escaped me and suddenly I was being lifted into the air and settled onto the counter. He laced his hands through my hair and took control of the kiss. It became slower, teasing and I wriggled against him, wanting, needing more.

I forgot about Ethan.

"Dad?" Ethan's voice came down from upstairs and it felt like I'd been hit by lightning. I was brought back to earth with a bump.

Steven laughed as he pulled away from me and rested his forehead against mine. "What is it?"

"I've brushed my teeth."

"I bet you haven't," he muttered good-naturally under his breath. The comment made me smile. "I'll be right there," he called up. He brushed another kiss against my lips and his dark eyes were filled with unspoken promise. "I'll be back down in a minute. Don't go anywhere."

I gave him five minutes, grabbed my coat, and rushed out the door. I didn't want to leave them like this but there was no way they'd understand. They weren't part of my world. My world would corrupt them, and I didn't want that.

Chapter Ten

I was halfway down the road when I finally stopped running. I'd never felt so confused before. My lips and the rest of my body still ached from the pretty epic kiss I'd shared with Steven in the kitchen. I shouldn't have rushed out of there like that, without an explanation. It had been the coward's way and I'd wanted to stay. I closed my eyes and took a deep breath, letting the frigid air fill my lungs, using it to steady my racing heart.

If I went back to Blue Isis, my life would change dramatically, and it wouldn't be for the better. They wanted me to be Ruby Williams again, but I hadn't been her for a long time. I'd managed to put them in terrible danger, and I wouldn't put it past Blue Isis to use them to keep me in line. I had three options. Go back to Blue Isis, which wasn't one I even wanted to consider. I could run, but that would leave Steven and Ethan in danger. The last option was just stupid—I could go on the run and take them with me. At least if they were with me I could keep them safe until I found somewhere where Blue Isis wouldn't find them or me.

I opened my eyes. I knew what I had to do.

I ENDED UP WALKING to the outskirts of Echo Falls, just where the line of trees stopped, and the ground became flat. He sat on the boot of a car. The headlights were on, and they looked like the eyes of a monster. He smiled at me as I walked toward him like we were old friends, and he hadn't blackmailed me to be there. I needed to wait until I was close enough before I attacked. Working my telekinesis from a distance was an option, but for a refined attack, an attack that won a fight before it even started, I needed to be as close as possible. My palms were sweaty, and I unconsciously flicked my hands, casting off any sweat.

He noticed the movement, but he didn't comment on it. He assumed I was nervous, and I was but not the way he thought I hadn't killed anyone in a long time. I could have killed Joseph, but in the end, I hadn't. This was only going to play out one of two ways—either I killed him, or he killed me. I could honestly say I didn't know which one I preferred. If he killed me it meant Ethan and Steven would be safe. They'd eventually forget about the odd woman they'd taken into their home.

"You made the right choice." He sounded confident and cocky, and I fought the urge to hit him with a blast of fury, but I wasn't close enough yet. I needed to take a few more steps.

"I know."

He got up from his seat. His whole body was silhouetted by the lights of the car. The light reflected off the metal handcuffs in his hands. "Turn around." A spike of fear traveled through me. The move had to be quick. I made a fist with my hand and started to channel my anger and rage at my situation into it. "I said turn around." His tone was sharp, and I raised an eyebrow.

"You said you weren't scared of me."

"I'm not."

"You should be." I flattened my hand and pushed, hard. I didn't even touch him, the energy did. He flew high, up, and over the car and landed with a thud. I heard a scuffle as he got back to his feet. He brushed off the dirt from the road and sighed. He didn't look as winded as I hoped, or as scared.

"You do know I don't have to take you in alive. They just told me to come and retrieve you. They weren't specific."

I squared my stance. "I'm not afraid to die." The air around me dropped about ten degrees. *What the hell?* I saw a flash of white and darted to the left as the ice spike flew past my head.

"I told you, you're not the only one with gifts," he said smugly.

As he walked around the car, I crawled around it, trying to keep as much distance between us as possible. I needed to think quickly. I looked around for weapons but came up empty. A loud thud from above me made my heart jump into my throat. I spun around, poured the last of my energy into my fists, and aimed for where I hoped his kneecaps were.

A scream ripped through the air as something shattered under the force of the telekinetic blast. He fell toward me. It happened so quickly I couldn't get out of the way. His fist hit my face and suddenly all I could see were stars. I tasted something warm and bitter—he split my lip.

"You're a stupid bitch." He growled the words at me as he grabbed me by the throat. "I've had enough of this bloody job. Why do you guys always have to fight? Blue Isis isn't a fate worse than death."

"You haven't been there very long then." I spat the words out. *Kill me and finally end it.*

He smiled through the pain, and blood stained his teeth. *He must have bitten his tongue when he fell off the car.* "Do you think it ends here? Oh yeah, it's the end of the road for you, but you're not the only reason I'm in Echo Falls."

"Who else are you here for?" I asked as he loosened his grip on my throat. He wanted to gloat, and he couldn't do that if he killed me right away. How considerate of him.

"The boy. We want the boy."

My heart stopped. "Why do you want Ethan?"

"Because he's one of us. Either way, they've managed to escape Blue Isis' net for long enough. They're as good at hiding as you. You can imagine our surprise to find you both in the same place."

I'd thought I used up all my energy in my last blast, but as soon as he mentioned Ethan's name, white-hot rage filled me. I might have no idea why they wanted the little boy, but they weren't going to get their grubby little hands on him. I brought up my knee hard and it connected with whatever I'd broken earlier. His eyes rolled back into his head, and I flipped him off me, reversing our positions.

I grabbed the side of his head, keeping my fingers away from his mouth. I didn't want to end up losing a finger. "Okay, Iceman, did you tell them you found me?"

He snorted as he tried to fight me off. "Of course, I did. We've got your scent now. There isn't anywhere you can go where we can't find you."

"Good, I won't feel too bad for doing this then." I channeled my power into my hands and tried to mentally block out the screams. I only stopped squeezing when it finally stopped. I rolled off him and then lay next to the dead man. I flicked the blood off my hands.

It looks like I'm not the only one who's been keeping secrets.

Chapter Eleven

As I stumbled through Steven's front door, my feet decided they no longer wanted to carry me. I hit the floor. My whole body started to crash. I used all my energy in the fight, my eyes didn't even want to stay open. My body was shutting down all but the most vital body functions. It had been a long time since I'd worked my gift that hard and now I paid the price. Suddenly, I was picked up and held in a pair of arms that couldn't belong to anyone but Steven. I hoped I hadn't woken Ethan.

"Damn it, Selene. What happened to you?" I could barely hear what he was saying. It was like my brain had been wrapped in cotton wool, muffling everything he said.

I was lowered down and enveloped by a bed so soft it could have been a cloud. It didn't feel like the one I'd been using; it was softer and smelled of Steven. He brushed my hair away from my eyes. Then he skimmed his hands over my now bare arms. It showed how far gone I was if I couldn't even remember him taking off my coat. "What the hell hit you, a truck? I'm going to call for an ambulance. I'll be right back."

The pressure of him getting up from the bed snapped me out of my daze. "It isn't safe. Please, Steven, just let me sleep for a little while and get my strength back. When I wake, I think it's time that we all sit down and talk."

I WOKE UP TO ANOTHER hand on my forehead. it wasn't Steven's. It felt too papery, too thin and the smell was almost chemical and harsh instead of the warm, musky male scent that tickled my nose and seeped into my bones. I sat up so fast I went dizzy. The person who stood over me took a step back and I noticed it was the woman from the information center.

"It's June, right? What are you doing here?"

"Helping you, it seems. What happened? And for the record, it's best if you just tell me the truth. I'll know if you're lying." She folded her arms across her chest.

"And how would you know if I'm lying?"

She looked at me wryly. "You're not the only gifted one in this town, Ruby."

My heart skipped a beat. Every time I heard my real name, someone either tried to blackmail me or kill me. My body was still weak and a part of me felt stupid about fearing a little old lady, even if she did know my real name. I told her the truth and understanding filled those watery blue eyes. When I was finally finished, she sat in one of the chairs.

"That explains a lot." She said from her seat.

"Really?" I asked in disbelief. "Because it only makes more questions for me. I knew they were after me, but why are they after Ethan?" I scrambled out of Steven's bed and nearly lost my balance. "Damn, how long was I out?"

June waved a hand as if that was all it took to dismiss my worries. "Steven is already packing a bag and a few things for the three of you."

I made my way around the room, my body screamed in protest as I fought to keep myself steady. I collected my boots and the jacket I borrowed from Steven when I left the night before. "He knows they want Ethan?"

She nodded. "He wanted a normal life. Unfortunately, he didn't realize helping you would change that."

I couldn't help the pang of guilt which rippled through me, but I pushed it away. There wasn't anything I could do about it now. "What can we do?"

"Run," she replied simply. "Echo Falls worked as a sanctuary for some of the Gifted, but you coming here disrupted that and a lot of them have fled. There's somewhere else, another haven. You'll be heading there. The little boy is important, Ruby. You've got to keep him safe."

I would keep him safe until I stopped breathing. I'd been wondering what it was about the solemn, brown-eyed boy which called out to my protective instincts, instincts I thought I never had to begin with. A part of me had known he was special, my kind of special, and even before the man had told me.

She shuffled over to the bed, sat down, and patted the duvet next to her, a silent invitation. "I'm one of the first Gifted. When I turned sixteen, I enrolled in a program for scientific testing. They did something to me which changed my genetic DNA."

"You were one of the originals?" I couldn't believe it. I'd heard of them, but I'd never thought I would meet one.

The prim and proper old lady shrugged; the movement odd on her. "I'm the only one to survive in my test group. As soon as I realized what they'd done to me, I ran. The others, the ones from different test groups followed me and I founded Echo Falls."

"I'm sorry, June. I didn't mean to bring them here."

She patted my hand. "It isn't your fault. Something about you being here shifted the protective layer over the town. You're telekinetic, aren't you?"

I nodded. "Could that have something to do with it?"

"So, you're awake." Steven walked into his room, and I couldn't meet his eyes. It wasn't just because I'd effectively screwed up his son and his life. It was the kiss. I hadn't blushed in a long time, but even now my cheeks heated from the memory. Just behind him, I spied an excited Ethan.

"Morning. Daddy told me about the road trip. Are you coming with us?"

"I told you she was. Now, go downstairs and have some breakfast. We'll be down in a minute."

I waited until Ethan got downstairs. "We don't have to all go together. It might even be better if we split up." I glanced at June. "It might be safer for them."

She looked at me skeptically. "Are you seriously trying to tell me you, the trained assassin, wouldn't be able to keep them safe?"

Her question riled me. "Of course, I can keep them safe."

"Then there shouldn't be a question of you helping them."

I DIDN'T TALK TO STEVEN as he drove. Instead, after I'd finally managed to relax without seeing people in every shadow, I let Ethan's enthusiasm sweep over me. I'd never seen him look so excited, so different from the shy boy who'd sat with me at the table the first night I stayed in the shed.

"Besides school, I've never really left Echo Falls," he informed me as we traveled. He stared out of the window with big eyes and my heart went out to him. He knew he was different, but I doubted he knew the real reason we were leaving town.

Steven had brought a few things from the house. There were three suitcases in the boot and two reasonable-sized boxes. One had Ethan's toys and books in it. Ethan didn't know we wouldn't be coming back yet, but Steven had packed enough of his things it wouldn't be a complete shock.

The other box held food and some drinks. We'd both agree it would be safer if we only stopped a few times.

After three hours, we pulled up at a gas stop. Steven took Ethan to use the toilet and I stretched my legs. To anyone who saw us we looked like a family. The thought had an odd effect on me. I couldn't deny that it wasn't a bad thought, but the idea of being a part of a makeshift family terrified me. It was up to me to keep them safe. I'd never had that responsibility before. Steven hadn't talked to me in the car. He had to blame me for leading Blue Isis to their door, however unintentional it had been. He expected me to be able to protect his son because of that mistake.

I'd rather die than let him be dragged into my world.

Steven brought Ethan back out, they were holding hands while they walked over the road toward me. Steven was slightly stooped over, making it easier for them to keep in contact. Ethan smiled at me widely and reached for my hand. As if working on instinct, I took it. Steven glanced across at me, and for a second he didn't look annoyed or angry, but happy.

Chapter Twelve

When I glanced up into the rear-view mirror the only thing I could see was Ethan cuddled up with a teddy bear, fast asleep. I fought the urge to turn around in my seat and push a strand of hair away from his face.

The silence wasn't comfortable. We needed to start talking to each other, even if it was just to keep him awake. "If you want to pull over I can drive for a while if you need to sleep."

He peeked at me from the corner of his eye, keeping most of his attention on the road. "Since Ethan's asleep it might be a suitable time to talk."

"Okay. Why don't we talk about Ethan then?"

A sharp intake of breath in response made me realize he'd been hoping for a slow start to the conversation. I had a habit of diving right in. "He's a third-generation healer. A little like June, but a lot more powerful. I've seen him bring a cat back to life. He knows he's different, even if I've tried to keep it away from him." He glanced in the rear-view and at his sleeping son. "He's so young. I thought I might have a few more years."

"But I managed to screw that up for you," I said watching the world pass by.

"Selene, you can't think like that. You didn't know you'd end up leading them to us. You didn't know Ethan is like you. I'm angry, but I don't blame you. I blame them."

A creak from the steering wheel drew my attention to Steven's white knuckles. "You're not one of us, are you?"

"No, it had been Ethan's mother who'd been gifted. We'd met in college, both training to be doctors. Georgina had always been talented. She could just look at people and figure out what was wrong with them. She never considered herself to be special, just a talented doctor. We got married and found out she was pregnant with Ethan. That's when Blue Isis approached us. At first, they tried to recruit Georgina. When she said no, they'd seemed okay with it. We later figure out they'd been waiting until she would be at her weakest."

I could understand that. She'd be focussed on giving birth and in no shape to run when they came for her. "What happened?"

Steven laughed, a soft sound that didn't wake his son. "She fought them anyway. I was called out of the delivery room. I didn't know anything was wrong until I saw Georgina pushing her way through a group of doctors and men in suits. She was brandishing an IV drip stand like a staff. I got her to the car, and I thought we'd managed to escape. I'd never been more scared. She'd been in full-blown labor on the backseat and there had been a car behind us. They tried to ram us off the road." He breathed in sharply as if he relived the memory of that horrible night..

I reached out, touching his hand on the steering wheel. He took his hand off it and laced his fingers through mine. It didn't mean anything; it didn't have the heat or the intensity of the kiss in the kitchen. I just wanted to comfort him. He'd gone through a lot. Both had.

"We went off the road. She'd been seriously hurt, and I managed to deliver Ethan before they got to us. She told me to run and said she'd slow us down. I cuddled our new-born son, wrapped up in my jacket, grabbed the bag which had her overnight stuff, and ran. That was the last time I saw Georgina alive." His brown eyes were shiny with tears and as he blinked they rolled down his cheek.

I squeezed his hand. "Could she still be alive?"

"No. Ethan's gifts are linked with his power to heal. If he thinks about someone hard enough, he can tell if they're dead or alive. One night a few years back, he woke up and came into my room. He told me mummy had died. It broke my heart. If I'd known she'd still been alive, I'd have tracked her down. I'd been so sure she died that night."

I didn't have anything to say. I rubbed a thumb over his knuckles. "You couldn't have known."

"I should have."

We drove on in silence. He never let go of my hand.

I WATCHED THE SUNRISE. I'd driven for the last couple of hours after I'd managed to get Steven to sleep. He was gently snoring, his head resting on the cold passenger side window. Ethan was still asleep, but I suspected he'd be awake soon.

The roads were deserted. The sky had an amber shade that showed the sun would appear soon. Everything was flat. There weren't any hills in the distance I could see. Spending my time growing up in cities or running away from them, the scenery had never seemed so desolate. Besides my sleeping passengers, the universe could have vanished in a blink of an eye, and we'd never have known.

Wow, I didn't think I'd ever felt so depressed before. I blamed it on my lack of sleep and too much coffee from the flask Steven had packed. A yawn brought my attention to the backseat. The little boy scooted forward, and I caught his silhouette between the two chairs. There wasn't enough space for a child seat but there was a booster seat, one that he'd managed to get free of.

"Morning sleepyhead," I aimed for sounding cheerful. I didn't agree with Steven not telling him the truth. Okay, he might be young, but lying to him didn't sit well with me. But then, I wasn't his mother. I didn't have any right to do it for Steven.

"Morning. Where are we?"

"On a very long road to the small town of Haven." June hadn't known if my telekinesis would throw off the protective bubble surrounding the town. It didn't matter though if Ethan and Steven were safe. I planned on leaving them there and running anyway.

"Are we going to stop for a break? I need to go to the toilet."

I promised we'd stop soon, and Steven stirred in his sleep. He'd wake up soon as well. We'd have to do another swap at the rest stop and I'd be able to get some sleep.

All I wanted to do was relax. I didn't know if they were tracking me. Every second that Ethan and Steven were with me, the more danger they were in. June had been so sure I would be able to keep them safe until we got to Haven. I hoped she was right. I would never forgive myself if something happened to them.

ETHAN DARTED OFF TO the loos at the rest stop, as Steven went into the store to buy more coffee. I guarded the car; sitting on the warm bonnet as I waited for them to get back. If I hadn't been there I wouldn't have seen the people pop into existence. As soon as I saw them I knew that they were Blue Isis. There were five of them, and they quickly moved behind the petrol gas station and the toilets. I had no clue how they found us. I also didn't know how they managed to just appear out of smoke. I'd never seen anything like that when I'd been with Blue Isis.

I ran forward. If I couldn't see them I was sure they couldn't see me. I needed to get to Ethan. I heard a creak and the door to the toilets opened. I poured my power into my closed fist. It's only when I saw the little head of dark hair, that I saw the two operatives a few feet away.

"Ethan, get down!"

I trusted he'd heard and understood me. I pulled my fist back, my telekinesis settled in it. As I followed through with my fist, I released it.

If I had time I'd have admired the result. The air moved, rippled, and then took them off their feet. The air curled like it had a life of its own. Leaves spired up like they were caught in a mini hurricane.

I was still running as I scooped Ethan up with my left arm, turned, and headed back to the car. I managed to readjust him, holding him close to my body, keeping him as safe as possible. The door to the store opened. I didn't even brave a look. All I could think of was getting Ethan into the car and away from here.

How the hell had they managed to find us?

"Selene?"

Steven sounded confused, and I'd lost track of the other three of the Blue Isis Group. So far none of them had reveal any gifts. I didn't want them to give them the time to go some show and tell. There was a heavy thud somewhere behind me. I don't know if it was the group, but I was hoping that it was Steven.

I circled the car. Looking over the bonnet I could see Steven rushing towards the car as well. Behind him, there was a woman with fists on fire. "Cover your ears, Ethan."

The little boy was curled up near my feet and quickly followed my orders. I stood and poured more energy into my hands and then pushed. I aimed slightly to Steven's left and managed to hit the little fire starter dead center. The screams were deafening. The air fed the fire coming from her hands and quickly spread all over her body. *The woman wasn't as flame retardant as her hands were.*

Steven opened the driver's side door and dived in. I picked up Ethan and got in with him on the back seat. I glanced out the back window; a faint tremor went through the little boy tucked up in the crook of my arm. I glanced behind me, through the window. Where were they?

I looked up and into the rear-view mirror; Steven quickly glanced at me before turning his attention back to the road. We had to get to Haven fast and we couldn't stop anymore until we did.

Chapter Thirteen

I kept my body turned to the back window. The road was empty behind us, but it had been that way before. I should have been happy they weren't there, but it raised an interesting question: why weren't they chasing us? How had they found us to begin with? After a little while, Ethan detached himself from me. The tremors which shook his body had finally stopped. As we sped away, Steven hadn't spoken a word. He was as nervous as me, scared.

"Are they after me?" Ethan said the words so softly that I nearly missed them.

Steven thought he'd have more time to tell Ethan the truth. Unfortunately, it had been taken out of his hands. Ethan knew that he was special, but he didn't know how much. His father had sheltered him the best way he could.

I caught Steven staring at me using the rear-view mirror, his dark eyes pleading. He didn't know what to say. It meant it was up to me. I was the closest person who knew what the boy was going through. I gently pulled Ethan until he rested against my side. It wasn't my place to tell him, to destroy whatever childhood he had left. It didn't look like I had much of a choice. I didn't want to rob him of his childhood. It wasn't fair.

"Originally, they were after me. I was born with a special gift. You saw what I did back there? It's called telekinesis and I used it for an exclusive group that wanted me to do unbelievably terrible things until I left them. They want me back."

The little boy's eyes went wide. I guess he hadn't known that some of the people in Echo Falls had been gifted as well. How many lives had

I ruined without even meaning to? I didn't linger on the thought. If I thought about all the people, I killed because of Blue Isis I'd never sleep again. "You're like me?"

"Our gifts might be different, but yeah, we're alike. We're traveling to a town where you and your dad are going to be safe."

"Why do they want me?"

I slowly brushed my fingers against his hair. "It doesn't matter, Ethan. They are never going to get you. I promise and I always keep my promises." Even if I had to do something terrible to make sure I kept them.

I glanced up and met Steven's eye in the mirror. He nodded at me in silent thanks, and I smiled at him. I envied the little boy. He was lucky he had a parent who loved him. I never knew if my parents were like that, if they'd known about the tests ran on their unborn baby and didn't care, or if they didn't know at all.

He'd been lucky he had a father who cared about him, willing to do anything to keep him safe.

Now, he had two people. I just had more firepower.

THE HOURS TICKED BY slowly. The sun touched the horizon making the landscape appear otherworldly and beautiful. I was just admiring the view with Ethan curled up next to me when I noticed the road sign *Haven 6 miles*. I nearly missed it since the sign was partially hidden by trees. "Did you see that?"

"Yeah. Can't believe we're there. Do you know what you're doing? Are you coming into the town with us?" It was a tempting invitation. What would it be like to have a normal life, a normal relationship?

In all honesty, it had been all I could think about when Ethan had fallen asleep. I couldn't risk putting them in danger. What if I disrupted the protective barrier again? How many more lives would I end up ruining? My happiness wasn't worth it. "It would be safer if I didn't." Steven went quiet. "It isn't like I don't want to. I do. Blue Isis isn't going to give up on trying to find me and I've put you guys in enough danger."

"We could keep you safe."

The unexpected words made me look back out the window blinking back tears. "One day I might just come back." It was a beautiful lie, but I couldn't give him more than that.

"We'll miss you." There was an almost tangible sadness to his voice.

I'll miss you too. In such a brief time, they'd both gotten underneath my skin, as close to my heart as I let anyone. "If Haven is supposed to be safe, why is it even on the map?"

Steven shrugged. "We live in a strange world. I think some things we just must take on faith. Anyway, if June says this place is safe I believe her."

He had a point. June had the boy's best interests at heart. She wouldn't put him in harm's way.

"If we don't get a chance, I wanted to say thanks for talking to Ethan. It was a talk I thought his mother would have with him eventually, but it didn't work out that way. Do you have any idea how they found us?"

"I'm not sure. The group has grown its numbers. When I was there, there wasn't anyone who could teleport. Since they appeared when we stopped they might not be able to track us while we're moving."

"So, do you think they'll be able to appear when we get out of the car at Haven?"

"I don't know. It's possible that if the town has a protective barrier, they might not be able to teleport into it." The whole situation was unpredictable, and I didn't like it. There was a faint glow across the horizon in front of us. Where Echo Falls had been surrounded by trees, Haven didn't have that. Uneasiness hit me unexpectedly. "Can you feel that?"

Steven's hands shook on the steering wheel. "What is that?"

The hairs on the back of my arms stood on end. "I don't know, but it's what keeps the town safe. Keep driving."

Panic flooded inside me. I took shallow breaths and tried to not let it get to me. The tension was making me wish I could claw through the doors. I hated to think how Steven was dealing with it. Thankfully, Ethan still slept peacefully next to me.

"I think we're being followed."

"What?" I carefully turned in my seat and looked out of the window. I wanted him to be wrong. It sucked that he was right. The only thing the black car was missing was a license plate that said, "bad guys r us."

"It's them." I bit my lip Steven's knuckles were white again. Was he thinking about the night he lost his wife, the car chase that ended in her death? I risked one more look at Ethan; strands of black hair had strayed onto his forehead. It was unfair that someone as young and innocent as him was going through this. It shouldn't matter what gifts he'd been born with.

There wasn't any way we could outrun them as soon as we stopped they would be on us. I doubted the compulsion would make them turn around, especially with their prize in sight. It meant we might end up delivering a bunch of Gifted to them. The minutes ticked down, and as they did, we ran out of time. It took a second for me to come up with a plan, and a little more to work up the courage.

This was going to hurt, a lot.

I carefully laid Ethan on the back seat and climbed between the seats, sitting next to Steven. The road was deserted beside us and the men behind us. At least I wouldn't hurt anyone else with my act of stupidity. I edged close and pressed a kiss to Steven's lips. The fear in his eyes was quickly replaced by confusion. "Get to the town. Don't worry about me."

"Selene, what are you going to do?" He asked sharply.

"I'm going to keep my promise. Tell Ethan I said sorry." I opened the passenger side door, raised my fists, and then jumped, twisting my body in mid-air until I faced the approaching car and punched. I just had enough time to see the car flip before I hit the ground and blackness swallowed me.

Chapter Fourteen

The smell of burnt metal assaulted my senses and I wrinkled my nose. It was the only part of my body that didn't hurt. Every bone and limb screamed in protest. It felt like I'd broken everything. Seriously, who the hell jumped out of a moving car?

I contemplated opening my eyes, but the idea was at war with just curling up on the ground and going to sleep. Someone else decided for me as hands grabbed the front of my jacket and pulled me up. The tips of my shoes brushed against the ground and my arm was a ball of pain. Great. I'd managed to dislocate it, again.

"Ms. Williams, well if it isn't a pleasure to meet you." That didn't sound like the truth. Distaste dripped from every word.

I attempted to peek out from underneath eyelashes that weighed a ton. My eyes refused to focus. Whoever held me up was strong and I got the impression of broad shoulders and a scowl. There were four undistinguished shapes behind him.

I opened my mouth to call him a liar, but a cough tore through my body instead. It took a few seconds to get it under control and my chest went tight, as pain stabbed through me. Wonderful, was there anything I hadn't broken? "Who the hell are you?" Everything slowly came back into focus. Blood dripped down from a nasty cut on his forehead. He ignored it as it worked a path down near his eye. The white shirt he wore was stained with the red stuff.

He sneered at me before he shook me again. My brain rattled in my skull. If he kept that up I was going to throw up. I closed my eyes and prayed for the world to stop spinning. "It's Weston, but after tonight, you'll call me boss."

I glanced down at my feet and watched them sway. Weston held me out at arm's length, and he hadn't even broken a sweat. "I'm sorry."

Confusion flashed behind his dark eyes, and I got a good look at the lackeys behind him. Most of them I don't know, but then I noticed James. His left eye was swollen and there was a cut to his bottom lip. Guilt hit me hard. I hadn't wanted to hurt him, but they'd left me no choice. It had been them or the kid. Weston shook me again and for a split second, everything went back. "What are you apologizing for? The fact your little stunt killed one of my men or that you lost us the boy?"

I smiled. Then it had been worth it. Every part of my body would hate me in the morning, but at least Ethan was free. "I'm sorry, but it'll be a freezing day in hell before I call your boss." I spat out some blood and it landed on Weston's expensive shoes with an audible splat. Suddenly, I hit the ground and blackness ate my vision. The hard pavement didn't make a comfortable pillow, and nobody bothered to pick me up. These guys held a grudge. I didn't blame them since I had killed more than one of their own.

"Get her in the car. At least we're not going back empty-handed."

"You want to be the one to tell Madame that we lost the boy?" As my body slipped into shock James' voice sounded farther away. I'd put my body through hell. I didn't have the right to complain when it started to rebel.

"Shut up, James," Weston replied sharply. "If you hadn't lost her, to begin with, we wouldn't be a man down."

A strong pair of arms scooped me up. The smell of aftershave pulled me back from the brink. It was familiar and my eyes flickered open. I turned my head and glanced up the line of a firm chest. James risked a look down at me. "You should have kept running," he whispered.

"Well, I've never been too good at following orders," I muttered as the pain finally took me and I lost my grip on consciousness.

ETHAN AND STEVEN HAUNTED my dreams while I slept. In my dream they were constantly running, dogs nibbling at their heels. I hoped they stayed in the small town and that the group never found them. It would suck if I'd given up my freedom for nothing. A life on the run, always looking over your shoulder wasn't a life I'd wish on anyone, but I would wish this life in the compound even less.

I'd slipped in and out of sleep. James had carried me as the elevator had traveled down the levels to the underground compound. When I woke up again he was laying me down on a bed. The briefest touch of his fingers against my cheek was the last thing I remembered before I slipped into darkness again.

A few hours must have passed before a doctor came into my room. She was alone, but that didn't mean much in the grand scheme of things. I wasn't in any fit state to fight her and even if I did, where would I go? The security had been beefed up since I'd been here last.

The mattress dipped next to me, and practiced hands touched my arms, legs, and my forehead. I kept my eyes closed as if I could fool her into thinking I was still asleep. All the time she did this I heard a scrape of pencil on paper as she noted each wound. I nearly yelped in surprise as she started to rub something cold against every cut.

I risked opening my eyes.

"Afternoon." Oh crap, there was something familiar about her, it took a while for my brain to catch up. I'd seen this woman before, she hadn't worked for the Group before I'd left. "My name is Doctor Henderson."

"It's Georgina, isn't it?" I pushed the words out of my mouth. There were a few more lines around her eyes, tiredness that was a result of working for Evil Incorporated, but it was her, the woman in the photograph in Steven and Ethan's living room.

Her gaze went wide in surprise. "How do you know my name?"

I was about to tell her when the door opened. The confused look hadn't left her eyes, I didn't miss how it quickly became indifference as James walked in. "I know Ethan and Steven." There was no point in mentioning how close I'd gotten to her family or the fact I'd kissed her husband. I was looking to make allies not more enemies.

She stopped as James walked further into the room; he carried in a small pile of clothes. "You must be wrong. My husband and child are both dead." I could almost sense the sadness in her voice.

"They're not dead."

Georgina half-turned and she was about to walk back to me when James touched her arm. I caught the look that passed between them—the precise moment Georgina realized I might be telling the truth. "You must be wrong," she said again looking at James, then back at me. She quickly vanished back through the door.

"How are you feeling?"

"Like I jumped out of a moving car?" I said as I collapsed back onto the bed. I shielded my eyes with my hand. I could hear him as he walked toward me and dumped my clothes onto the bottom of the bed. "What was in that stuff that she rubbed into me?"

James laughed softly. "Trust me, you don't want to know." The smile quickly vanished from his face. "I told you to run."

I "I had to stop eventually." I didn't bother going into too much detail. I didn't know what game James played. We'd been friends, lovers, and enemies. He'd helped me to escape, but I was sure he wouldn't be helping me again anytime soon.

"They'll want to know where the boy is."

I shrugged and tried for a smile. "That's a shame since I don't know."

"Selene..."

"I don't know, James, but even if I did I wouldn't tell them."

Chapter Fifteen

My body might have started to feel normal and less like I'd thrown myself out of a moving car, but from the way, Weston cracked his knuckles it was obvious he wanted to put me back into the hospital wing. Jeez, you throw up on a guy's shoes once and he holds a grudge forever. They'd tied me to a chair, my hands slid through a gap cut into the back of it and held in place with cuffs. The metal cut into my wrists but I'd survived worse pain. They wanted me nervous, on edge. I had to admit they succeeded, a little. I kept my nerve though. I knew how the game was played. It was just my first time in the chair.

Weston leaned against the wall in front of me. A much smaller guy sat behind me. There was a pull in the pit of my stomach as he worked as a power siphon. They were a regular part of the interrogation process. During my time in the Group, I tried not to spend much time in their company. They had no control over their powers and any real-time around them left a person feeling queasy.

The door next to Weston opened and a woman who wore a suit that cost more than my flat waltzed in like she owned the place. Everything about her screamed power and common sense said I should listen to what she had to say. With Weston's strength, my body parts might start lining the floors if I pissed her off. Unfortunately, I doubted that message would get through to my brain. When trapped in a room without access to my powers and an attitude a mile wide, this was only going to end one way. Unless I did the unexpected, I wouldn't be walking out of the room. They might not kill me, but I didn't like my chances.

"I would call you Ms. Williams, but I hear you don't go by that name anymore."

I tried to shrug, but my trapped arms made the movement difficult. "It's Selene Ryder now. I don't think we've met." During our little exchange, Weston had moved from his position on the wall to behind me. I didn't like not being able to see him. The woman gave a slight nod and I saw stars. Due to the power siphon, I knew Weston couldn't hit me with his full strength, but damn if it didn't still hurt like a bitch.

"We haven't." There was a curve to her lips that could have been mistaken for a smile if her eyes weren't cold. "Now, I'm going to ask you a few questions. It depends on your answers if you get to walk out of here. Tell me something I don't want to hear, and Weston will start breaking bones. Am I clear? I do hate to repeat myself."

I waited until my double vision cleared before I risked looking up at her. "I'm not going to be much use with my brain scrambled."

"That's why I decided on breaking bones instead. Pain can be a wonderful motivational tool. Now, tell me where Ethan is."

They had to start with a hard one. "I don't know."

The woman studied me with careful eyes as if she could catch me in a lie. "Well, that's a shame." She glanced over my shoulder at Weston, who hadn't moved. "Break one of her fingers."

"Gladly." I didn't have to see him to know he was smiling. Any opportunity for inflicting pain had that effect on him.

"Wait!" I jerked away from the man behind me but knew it was pointless. I wouldn't be getting out of the chair unless they let me go. "I thought you were after me?"

The mysterious woman raised a hand. Weston stopped next to my chair. "You were the target, but Ethan? He's an enigma, a product of a relationship between a norm and a Gifted. Imagine what it would be like to test him? To pull him apart and find out what makes him tick."

Sickness welled in the pit of my stomach. It had more to do with the fact she didn't think of him as a boy, a little boy who hated Math and had wide brown eyes. She thought of him as a weapon, something she needed to figure out. I knew what I had to do to do to keep him safe. "You'll never find him." They would find him. Something would happen to put him back on their radar. It might take weeks, months, or years, but it would happen. No one stayed hidden forever.

"I like a challenge." She smirked; her arms crossed.

"I have a proposition for you."

Her laugh was mocking. "You're not in any position to be making deals."

I glanced around at the siphon, Weston, and the woman in front of me. Yeah, I was officially in a tricky situation. I couldn't let it stop me though. They needed me. They'd searched for three years to get me back and they'd prefer me to join up willingly. All it had taken was a threat towards Ethan for me to change my whole die-before-I-came-back-here stance.

"I'm offering my services. Ethan doesn't have any powers and if they do make an appearance, it might not be for years. If you grab him now, you'll raise questions. He's a child; people aren't just going to let you take him. On the other hand, I've worked for you before. I'm good at my job and I'll join you willingly, as long as you let Ethan go."

She smiled. "You've changed since you left us. Are you sure that you can still do the job?"

I wanted to kill her as much as I wanted my next breath. "It'll be like riding a bike."

She was seriously considering it; I could read it in her eyes.

"As long as you don't touch Ethan, I'll play the role of perfect little assassin."

"I could just kill you." The look in her eyes harden.

"Where's the fun in that?" For a split second, I thought I pushed it too far as a heavy hand fell onto my shoulder.

She sighed and I caught the disappointment in her eyes. "I wanted to torture you. There was a plan and everything. I was going to make you bleed." There was a slight sway to her hips and a dreamy look chased away the disappointment.

Now, that's odd. At that moment, she looked like a completely different person. "Madame?" Weston squeezed my shoulder so hard I winced. More bruises to add to the collection.

The dreamy look vanished. "If you step out of line, Ms. Ryder, I'll have a bullet put into you."

"Thanks for not sugar-coating that."

She smiled. "I thought you'd appreciate the honesty. Weston, escort her back to her room please."

I fought against the urge to massage my wrists when the cuffs were taken off. Weston gripped my shoulder and tugged me to my feet. I risked a glance at his shoes and smirked. The shiny pointy ones had been replaced with more sturdy boots that didn't match his suit. He'd thrown out the other pair. I kept my mouth shut as he escorted me down the hall. The corridor was empty besides the windows that opened into rooms filled with office equipment and people who talked into headsets. None of them looked up as we walked past. A push to the shoulder had me tumbling against the wall. I hadn't been walking fast enough for my well-groomed and pissed-off boss. My cheek grazed against the wall before I regained my balance.

"You keep touching me like that, Weston, and you're going to lose a finger."

Power slowly started to flood back into my body the further we got away from the siphon, but I wasn't in any shape to fight him. Instead, I fell back on my old reliable. If only my wit was as sharp as an actual knife.

"You'll fuck up. We both know it. The only way you're leaving this place is in a body bag." The words were hissed against the curve of my neck.

I bit back a laugh. "You steal those lines from a Bond villain?" I was more worried about throwing up again as I was spun around and pinned to the wall. It wouldn't take much for him to pull me apart.

"I will have respect, Ryder, or I'll kill you without Madame's okay." He scanned my face. There's no mistaking the distaste on his. "You might have been a brilliant assassin in your day, but a lot can change in three years. If you don't prove yourself useful, it won't matter. She'll kill you anyway."

The pressure of his hands on my shoulders made me want to grit my teeth. "I'm glad we're on the same page, but let's make sure that we're clear. If you touch me again, I'll rip off your arm and bash you to death with it. Are we clear?" I used the voice, the part of me closely tied to the assassin. If it came to a fight between the two of us, I would be the only one to walk away from it. Even if it took every ounce of strength I had.

The smile matched his dead stare. "I think you'll try."

I managed to stay on my feet as he let me go. Weston might need to touch me to use his strength on me, but I sure as hell didn't. I just needed a valid reason. Madame wouldn't appreciate me killing one of her men, but if it was between him and me? There would be no holding back.

I kept my dark thoughts to myself as Weston escorted me the rest of the way to my room. The scowl on his face made me feel better; it was the petty things to help me get through the day. I was left at the door. My hands shook, it wasn't fear. It was the adrenalin that pumped through my veins. Closing my eyes, I took a few deep breaths to slow down my heart rate ran through my chest.

In less than a week, I'd made an enemy. That was quick even for me. It might have been quicker if I hadn't been unconscious for a part of it. I sat down on my bed, pulled my sweater up and over my head, and collapsed back onto it. It was like I'd never left, but things had changed. James was still there, that was complicated, it always had been, even more now he and Georgina had something going on. I wondered how long that would last since I mentioned her husband and child were still alive. I'd caught the guilt in her eyes. It might have been reflected in mine as well. I'd shared a kiss with her husband. At least Ethan was safe. I hoped he had plenty of years ahead of him growing up, leading a normal life.

The world kept spinning and I had people to kill. It was a twisted place I lived in, one jaded assassin for the safety of a little boy. I could live with that, which was good since I no longer had a choice.

The End

When a dragon horrifically murders his companions, the wizard Yosef quits his life as an adventurer. Instead of spells, he conjures sweet cakes and breads in his bakery. Instead of treasure, he opts for coin. And instead of magical shields, he dons a grouchy mantle to avoid any and all personal connections. He is quite happy never to go on an adventure again. The daughter of a dragon and a human man, Ayako attracts trouble like a magnet. A run-in with an orc leads her to the wizard Yosef. Her empathic ability reveals there's more to this man than his grumpy outer shell.He wants to keep his previous life a secret. She longs for a life without the complication of being half dragon. Unfortunately, trouble isn't far behind, and they both need to face their pasts if they hope to have a future.